James H. Graff, Bracebridge Hemyng, Lascelles Wraxall

The Nobleman on the Turf

In Bad Hands

James H. Graff, Bracebridge Hemyng, Lascelles Wraxall

The Nobleman on the Turf
In Bad Hands

ISBN/EAN: 9783337412395

Printed in Europe, USA, Canada, Australia, Japan

Cover: Foto ©Andreas Hilbeck / pixelio.de

More available books at **www.hansebooks.com**

THE

NOBLEMAN ON THE TURF;

OR,

IN BAD HANDS.

BY

SIR HENRY WRAXALL, BART.,

AND

BRACEBRIDGE HEMYNG.

LONDON:
CHARLES H. CLARKE, 13, PATERNOSTER ROW.

LONDON
HEAD, HOLE & CO., PRINTERS, FARRINGDON STREET, E.C.

THE NOBLEMAN ON THE TURF;

OR,

IN BAD HANDS.

CHAPTER I.

CASTLE COMPTON.

CASTLE COMPTON had for years been the chief seat of the Dukes of Masborough. The title of the first duke of that name dated far back in the fifteenth century. The dukedom was a rich one and had estates attached to it, with long rent rolls, in various parts of England. Probably the income was nearly 100,000*l.* a year, which even in these days of large commercial fortunes is sufficient to entitle an aristocrat to respect. The young Duke of Masborough at three-and-twenty was a standing example of the evils of primogeniture. If there had been no law of that description, the property would have long ago been split up amongst his uncles and granduncles, and probably been of more use to the State than it was in his hands. But the knell of the law of primogeniture and entail has not yet sounded.

Arthur Arundel Masham, Duke of Masborough, came into the title at the early age of fifteen, when he was at

B

Eton. His father, who had held various leading positions in the country, owing to the influence which the noble old Whig families can always command, to the exclusion of better men, made an esteemed friend and member for the county of Cheshire, in which Castle Compton was situated, his guardian. Mr. Ommaney Lane Whittaker, M.P., was a person totally unfitted for the post, for though well-meaning, he had little strength of mind, and detested anything which gave him the least trouble, which is a peculiarity not confined to members of the Commons' House, as it is the fashion to call the first club in London.

The Duchess of Masborough was very fond of her child, and, as a matter of course, spoilt him in the most egregiously absurd manner, letting him have his own way in everthing and do very much as he liked. At the age of eighteen he went up to Oxford from Eton, and evinced no inclination to take a degree; the little knowledge he had acquired at Eton just enabling him to matriculate, and at Oriel he did his best to forget what he had already learnt. We need scarcely add that in this laudable endeavour he was as highly successful as his sincerest admirers could wish.

After three years' stay at Oxford, he signalised himself one fifth of November by an exploit, in which the destruction by burning of a college pump in a quad was the principal feature, and it was deemed advisable by his mother and guardian to withdraw him, for a time at least, from that ancient and classic seat of learning, as he showed a stronger disposition for fighting bargees and riding in steeple-chases, than he did for the acquisition of Greek, Latin, and the higher mathematics.

Foreign travel was suggested. It usually is in such cases, and it was determined that he should, like Lord Lovell in the song, 'Go foreign countries for to see.' (Chorus *ad libitum.*) The next thing was to find him a fit and proper travelling companion, and at his own particular request a gentleman, whose acquaintance he had made at Oxford, and who belonged to one of the Halls and had just taken his Master's degree, was selected as his travelling tutor, at a salary of five hundred a year and his expenses.

The gentleman's name was Stoney Hines. No one knew much about his family. He had gained an exhibition at some provincial school, and so gone up to the University, aided by a small allowance from his father, it was said, and it was further whispered that his father was, or had been, a gaol chaplain somewhere in the South of England. No one could say, however, that Mr. Stoney Hines was a fool. His enemies, and he was sufficiently individualised and clever to have many, admitted that he was a young man of brilliant genius, who had made his way at the University solely by his talents, which had gained him respect, if not esteem.

Neither the duchess nor Mr. Whittaker thought of inquiring about his principles or moral character. He was clever. He would coach Masborough and get him on. He could speak French and knew a little German, and was therefore admirably fitted for the young nobleman's companion. In addition to this, he was six or seven years older. Thirty is an age of discretion ; he would keep his volatile charge in check, and so they started together. The duchess gave her son her blessing, and Mr. Ommaney Lane Whittaker—he being just of age—gave him the unlimited control of his affairs, the power to spend an income of nearly ten thousand a month, and contented himself with advising him not to go ahead too much, although he admitted it was necessary that an English duke should keep up the reputation of his class abroad.

At the time our story opens, the Duke of Masborough and his tutor, Mr. Stoney Hines, had been absent two

years. The duchess had heard of them at almost every
part of Europe, and the Mediterranean coasts of Africa
and Asia. They had announced their intention of
returning home. It was in December, and they were
to arrive two days before Christmas. Castle Compton
put on an unwonted appearance of gaiety and bustle.
A select circle of friends (according to the *Morning
Post*) were invited to spend Christmas at the castle ;
the staff of servants was increased, and general preparations for rejoicing and being merry were made.
Among the guests who first arrived were Mr. Ommaney
Lane Whittaker, still M.P for the long-suffering
county of Cheshire. The constituency might have
found a more efficient member, but they shopily re-
flected that Mr. Whittaker was rich, and highly respectable, and owned a deal of land in the county, and,
besides that, his father had occupied the same position
before him. How *could* they turn him out after all
these qualifications for the post were taken into consideration ? The thing was clearly impossible. So
respectable imbecility as usual carried the day. With
Mr. Whittaker arrived Captain Douglass Arnott, and
his sister, Emily Arnott; their mother and father were
to follow on Christmas-day. The Arnotts were also
local celebrities, and landowners for nobody knew how
many generations. Mr. Arnott boasted that he would
give his daughter a *dot* of 50,000*l.* down on the nail
when she married, provided she did so with his consent,
and consequently the fortune hunters swarmed about
her like so many flies around a pot of honey. But
Emily Arnott remembered that, before Masborough
went abroad with Mr. Hines, he had told her, while
walking in the gardens of the castle, on a summer
evening, with his arm round her waist, and his eyes
burning into hers, that he loved her ; and she believed
him, and thought herself happy, for she too loved the

handsome young nobleman with all her heart and soul. Miss Arnott was young, pretty, and susceptible. Most fair-haired young ladies of nineteen, with baby faces, think love the Alpha and Omega of life, and she was no exception to the general rule. Certainly she was extremely attractive, and when the duchess saw the turn affairs were taking she was much pleased, hoping that her son might indeed marry Miss Arnott, whom she was quite willing to receive as her daughter-in-law. A mother does not always approve of her son's wife, either before or after marriage, and there must have been something very agreeable about Emily to induce her to regard her with so much favour. But she had known her and her friends all the girl's life, and that made a difference, perhaps.

At first Masborough wrote often to Miss Arnott, and his letters contained expressions of affection which her soul fed upon as the gods drank ambrosia. After a time his communications were not so frequent, and their tone grew colder. To account for this change she was utterly at a loss. She could not accuse herself of any fault. She grew uneasy, and became miserable when Masborough told her that he was going to make a journey to Mecca, and could not give her any address to write to. After this she heard no more from him. In subsequent letters to his mother he said—'Remember me very warmly to Emily,' and, later on, 'Give my kind regards to Miss Arnott,' or, 'How are the Arnotts? Do you see much of them? Remember me when you meet.' Emily had many a good cry in secret over this coldness and neglect, but she was too proud to show openly what she felt. The duchess, however, felt for her, and tried to comfort her.

'He is young, and a little wild, dear,' she would say. 'He hates writing letters, and calls it a bore. You will not find him changed when he comes back. Pray excuse him for his carelessness, I am sure he does not mean it.'

So Emily hoped against hope, and waited anxiously for the day of his return. When she was told that he was expected at Christmas, and she received an invitation to meet him, how her heart fluttered. It was all she could do to restrain her nervous anxiety, which threatened to make her seriously ill.

On the morning of the day which he had fixed for his arrival, the Duchess of Masborough and Mr. Ommaney Lane Whittaker held a consultation in the boudoir of the former.

'I am so glad Masborough is coming home,' began the duchess. 'It is so long since he was here that I confess I am quite anxious to see him again. He will be no longer the fair boy, with the slender moustache.'

'Certainly the sun will have browned him a little, and he will be all the more manly for having seen the world,' answered Mr. Whittaker; 'yet I do not expect to see him much altered, except in a certain gravity which he ought to have acquired.'

'He ought to think of settling. This is the age of early marriages ; the Royal Family set the example.'

'Who could he have except his old love ? '

'Miss Arnott? Emily is a dear, good girl, and in every way worthy of him, though he has not taken so much notice of her lately as I could have wished,' replied the duchess thoughtfully.

'Carelessness always was his great fault,' observed Mr. Whittaker.

'Yet his heart is good.'

'Oh, I believe that always was in the right place. If he follows in his father's footsteps he will take a high place in the ministry one of these days. I am tired of parliamentary life. If he had not a seat in the House of Lords I think I should resign in his favour.'

'Any nominee of yours is sure to be elected, so that need not matter.'

'Positively certain,' returned Mr. Whittaker confidentially. 'No one could stand against our united interests.'

'If he would publish a volume of his travels it would attract notice, and do him some good, but he has no literary talent I fear.'

'That matters very little. There are many men in London to be got hold of who can and will write anything if they are paid for it. You have seen my pamphlet on Political Economy? well, I did not write a line of it. I merely gave a man the ideas, and got the credit of being a profound thinker and facile writer.'

Mr. Ommaney Lane Whittaker took a pinch of snuff, and chuckled as he thought how easily he had gulled the public generally, and his constituents in particular.

'Ours is quite a statesman-like name,' remarked the duchess.

'It has been so for generations.'

'I wish Masborough were a little more studiously inclined.'

'Most young men sow wild oats,' answered Mr. Whittaker, 'and I suppose he is no exception to the rule.'

'Let us hope he has finished sowing them,' the duchess said with a cheerful smile.

'It is not the sowing, my dear madam, that matters so much. It is the extent of the crop that has to be afterwards reaped,' remarked Mr. Whittaker, profoundly.

'Ah! precisely: but we must not indulge gloomy anticipations; let us hope for the best.'

'Certainly, let us hope. It can do no harm, and he is in good hands with Hines. Capital fellow, Hines!'

'And so clever.'

' Overwhelmingly so. Excellent fellow, Hines. Quite invaluable. Oh, here comes Captain Arnott !'

A gentleman about thirty entered the room, and apologised for his intrusion, saying, ' I really beg your Grace's pardon ; I was told I should find my sister with you, and I know she wants some commissions executed.'

' Don't mention it, Captain Arnott. Are you going to Chester ?' said the duchess.

' Yes ; I drive over in half-an-hour. Can I do anything for you, or for Mr. Whittaker ?'

Both responded in the negative.

' We were talking about Masborough, and saying what a capital fellow Hines is as a companion for him,' said Mr. Whittaker.

' Indeed !' said Captain Arnott, shortly.

' You do not seem to think so !' the duchess said, quickly.

' Well, frankly, I don't, and never did ; though I don't care about talking of a man behind his back.'

The duchess and Mr. Whittaker looked at one another as if it was high treason to entertain a doubt respecting the mental ability or moral character of Mr. Stoney Hines.

CHAPTER II.

THE EVIL GENIUS.

' I HAVE always regarded him as a man of high attainments and great promise. So steady ; such principle ; so clever !' said Mr. Ommaney Lane Whittaker, after a pause.

' And I, also,' chimed in her Grace.

' Well, he may be,' said Captain Arnott, hesitatingly. ' What you say induces me to regard him in a new light, though I must confess I should not like to have money on the event.'

' What do you know of him ?' said Mr. Whittaker.

' Nothing positively ; that is to say, of my own observation.'

' Now, I do beg of you, Captain Arnott,' said the duchess, ' to tell us anything you may have heard. Masborough is entirely in his hands, and if it is judicious to remove him, why it must be done.'

' All I know is, that he and my brother Charles were up at Oxford together. Mr. Hines is a Brazenose-man, so is Charles. Naturally we talked of Mr. Hines, when we heard he had gone abroad with Masborough. Charles says he is clever, but nothing else. He was a great gambler, and would make young fellows play at cards and pluck them. As for being steady, Charles says it is all nonsense ; for one night, when an attempt was made to blow up the statue of Cain and Abel in Brazenose quad, he saw Mr. Hines running away, and has no moral doubt that he was the culprit, though another man was sent away for it. He speculated, too, rather heavily, on all races at the University, and all turf races, having an especial fondness for Newmarket and horses. Still, he may have altered, and Charles may have been deceived. I am glad to be set right about Mr. Hines, though I will say that his deep, calculating face and cunning grey eyes are against him.'

' I have remarked the restless expression of his eyes,' said the duchess, evidencing that her confidence was waning, and showing how easy it is to prejudice one person against another.

' And now I come to think of it, I never liked his face; there was always something designing about it,' observed Mr. Whittaker.

' He must be got rid of.'

' I shall take an early opportunity of speaking very seriously to Masborough about it.'

' I hope no harm has been done as yet,' said the duchess.

' It would be an irreparable injury if Masborough should have imbibed any of his tastes and habits,' said Mr. Whittaker.

' I fear I have alarmed your Grace and Mr. Whittaker. If so, it was entirely unintentional on my part,' said Captain Arnott.

' Will you talk to my son when he arrives? You can do it as an old friend; that is, if you see anything wrong, and a man will have a better opportunity of judging,' said her Grace.

' Certainly I will. I shall consider it my duty since you have asked me,' the captain answered.

' Dear me ; how strangely things come about! I did not expect this ; candidly, I did not,' remarked Mr. Whittaker, taking a prodigious pinch of snuff from a handsome gold box, which had at one time belonged to George IV

'You acquit me of any prejudice in this matter?' the captain said.

'Of course, my dear Arnott; we know you are above that,' answered Mr. Whittaker, immediately; 'your communication is a favour. I assure you I regard it as such.'

'For my part,' said the duchess, 'I am personally indebted to Mr. Arnott.'

Then the conversation ended, but it left a strong impression upon the minds of all three. Arnott drove over to Chester. Her Grace went out in the carriage, and Mr. Ommaney began to read the *Times* which had just come down from London.

It was late in the afternoon when the Duke of Masborough, accompanied by Mr. Stoney Hines, arrived at the castle. The carriage had been waiting for him all day at the railway station. He was not above the middle height, stout, and rather heavy in appearance, with a fat face which might have concealed intelligence behind its pudginess, but allowed no scintillation to escape. He wore no beard, had a moustache and thin whiskers; his manner was reserved but not thoughtful, and his conversation did not betray any waste of time on thought or reading. Mr. Hines, on the contrary, was tall, thin, dark and quick, clean as to the absence of hair on his face, simple in attire as his Grace was loud, and something like a Jesuit priest in manner. We would try and find another simile, but cannot imagine one more forcibly conveying the disagreeable impression he produced on the beholder. The duke's manner was gentlemanly, easy, and well-bred; he greeted the friends assembled to meet him kindly, kissed his mother, and shook hands with Emily in a hearty manner, which disarmed her suspicions.

Christmas passed over, with a constant round of festivities. There was plenty of shooting in the well-

stocked preserves ; in the absence of frost, the hounds
met three times a week, and his Grace created a favourable impression by declaring his intention of accepting
the mastership, which the present holder of that position was desirous of resigning on the score of ill health,
though in reality because the expense was greater than
he could afford.

It was not until some of the guests had taken their
departure that Mr. Whittaker ventured to talk to the
young duke, who had delighted every one with his
varied stories of travel, his excellent shooting, the way
in which he flirted with and danced with the ladies,
the careless rate with which he lost money at cards
or billiards, and his devil-may-care manner generally—
when we say everybody we must except his mother. In
her anxious eyes he was by far too easy and careless ; he
seemed to live for pleasure only, and to seek for constant excitement, as if he wished to forget some unpleasant passage of his life, in the everlasting round
of pleasure. Mr. Hines was his shadow ; he was
always at his elbow, scarcely ever left him, accompanied him on all his rambles, and exercised a vast
and undoubted influence over him. To Mr. Whittaker
and to the duchess Hines was affability itself, to others
he was offhand and even rude, as if he felt his position
so secured that he could venture to assume a manner
which, coming from such a man, was to many insuffer-
ably offensive ; but he was quick at retort, clever in
sarcasm, and in a few hastily uttered words could wound
severely without saying anything which the hearer could
fix upon to make a quarrel ; so, while the duke was the
most popular man in the house, Mr. Hines was the one
most universally disliked.

Catching the young duke alone one morning, Mr.
Whittaker took advantage of the opportunity to talk
seriously to him.

After a preliminary 'break' his late guardian said, 'And what are your intentions, my dear boy?'

'About what?' asked Masborough, staring stupidly at the fire.

'Things in general—the course you intend to pursue?'

'That is soon answered,' replied the duke. 'The course I intend to follow is the race-course.'

'The what?' said Mr. Whittaker, paralysed with astonishment and gasping for breath.

'The turf, racing, and all that sort of thing; don't you understand? I have sixteen horses in training now at Chantilly I bought from Count Lagrange, and Hines is looking out, over here, for a trainer and some good quarters, as I mean to purchase largely, and must have some good entries for the races.'

'Mr. Hines is doing this?' said Mr. Whittaker, recovering himself.

'Certainly; he acts under my orders.'

'Then, all I can say is that Mr. Hines is acting most disgracefully, and is not fit for the position he has so long held; he has shamefully abused his trust,' said the guardian, allowing his indignation to explode.

'You had better tell him so,' the duke rejoined with a half smile.

'I shall certainly take an early opportunity of doing so, and in no measured terms. You have indeed astonished me. I could never have believed that you would have evidenced a liking for such a career. Think how many noblemen have been ruined on the turf!'

'I am at home in a stable, and I flatter myself I know the points of a horse as well as I do those of a woman,' said Masborough, quietly.

'Points of a horse—points of a—Bless me, what language is this? How unlike my poor dead friend, your father. But you must be joking,' said Mr. Ommaney Lane Whittaker.

'I! Oh, dear no! I assure you I never was more serious in my life. I will win a few Darbies and Sillingers if I live long enough.'

'Darbies and Sillingers!' said the poor guardian in despair, uttering a sort of wail. 'He talks of things like those when he ought to be considering the proposed measures for the pacification of Ireland, the advisability of adopting the ballot, the abolition of tests in the universities, our licensing system, and a dozen other great topics of the day.'

'Bother politics!' said his Grace, lighting his second cigar since breakfast, and helping himself to some curaçoa from a liquor case; 'I can't stand politics.'

'Can't stand politics? then you're not a Masborough; you are degenerate.'

'You need not be personal, Mr. Whittaker,' interposed the young man. 'I am sensible of the interest you take in my welfare, but believe me I am quite capable of looking after my own affairs without help even from you. I intend to keep race-horses.'

'In an assumed name?'

'In my own. Bentinck, Derby, Westmoreland, Stamford, Newcastle, and many others, have all done the same thing. I mean to hunt the county, and live like a country gentleman · of the Tatton Sykes kind. I should be out of my sphere in the political arena. I doubt if I could make a speech except after dinner, and then there would not be much in it. Do you find anything so very startling in the announcement?' asked the duke.

'Indeed I do,' replied Mr. Whittaker sadly. 'I see that you, whom I regarded with as much pride and affection as if you had been my own son, have made an evil choice; really you have. The great name, the histor/cal name of Masborough, instead of being mentione/l by millions with reverence and esteem, will be bandied about by turf swindlers and blacklegs. It will become a bye-word to all who have your welfare at heart, and a man in your position is the property of his country. You cannot do what you like with yourself, and—and—by God you shan't !'

The duke frowned, but made no answer.

' If I can help it you shall not touch this pitch, which will defile you. You owe it to my years to respect my advice. You owe it to your mother to halt before this abyss,' Mr. Whittaker went on, in the same emphatic manner.

' My dear sir, recollect that you are not speaking to a schoolboy, and I have no wish to quarrel with you, but——'

' Well, well, well, I must consult with your mother. This conversation has taken me by surprise,' said the old gentleman testily.

' If any of my friends should wish to have a lecture on the advantages to be derived from being a good boy I will refer them to you.'

' It is no laughing matter, my dear young friend, as you will find out to your cost some day. But I will speak with your mother.'

With these words Mr. Whittaker quitted the room hastily.

' You're off in a huff,' was the young nobleman's comment on his departure.

Oddly enough, as he went out at one door Mr. Hines entered at another.

' Oh, is it you, Hines ? ' said the duke. ' Whittaker has been here, giving me quite a moral sermon.'

' I heard every word of it,' answered Mr. Hines coolly.

' The deuce you did ! '

'Yes; the door was open, and——'

'You listened. I must compliment you on your mode of gaining information, but nothing comes amiss to you; I never saw such a fellow.'

'I don't mind what I do in your cause, as you know,' answered Mr. Hines. 'You have had proof of that before now. What would you have done at Baden if——'

'For heaven's sake don't recall that incident!' interrupted the duke hastily, as he averted his face; 'you know it makes me ill. I was a fool, and you got me out of the mess I was in, after a fashion of your own.'

'Precisely. You could not have stated the situation better,' answered Mr. Hines. 'And now with regard to Mr. Whittaker and his sage advice—what do you mean to do?'

'Do as I please, to be sure, and pursue a glorious career on the turf, as I have all along been determined.'

'You have a right to please yourself.'

'Of course I have. My ambition is to fill my sideboard with race-cups and trophies, won by my horses, and I mean to have the best blood in the world, if I pay ten times its weight in gold for it.'

'A laudable ambition,' answered Mr. Hines. 'Excuse me now, will you? I have some letters to write.'

'Shall you be ready in an hour? I mean to drive a tandem over to Chester,' asked the duke.

'I will be with you.'

Mr. Hines retired to his own apartment, and having closed the door muttered—

'I have him safe enough, though I rather feared their home influence. Such is *his* ambition. *Mine* is very different. When I have feathered my nest sufficiently, through his folly, I intend to stand for some borough, and get into Parliament. A man is nothing in this country without money. If he has none himself he should get it from others. I mean to do so. Once tolerably well off I will make a name for myself, and this poor fool may settle down with what is left to him, and shoot his pheasants, and hunt his foxes, and back the favourite, and I will back him, that is, I will ride on his back to fame and fortune.'

CHAPTER III.

EMILY ARNOTT.

THE Arnotts, who lived at Merrion Hall, in the same county, were very old friends of the Masboroughs, and whenever the young duke saw Emily Arnott, he felt an emotion which he could not disguise. An invitation given by Captain Arnott, her brother, to spend a week at Merrion, was readily accepted, and he went as soon as the festivities consequent upon his return home would admit of his going. He was rather glad of the opportunity, in fact, as he was constantly worried by the advice given him by his mother and Mr. Ommaney Lane Whittaker, who considered it their bounden duty to urge him to desist from a career which they felt would bring him no credit, and might materially damage his fortune and prospects in life. He had set his mind upon a sporting life, and on the turf he would go, so he contented himself with listening wearily to the homilies of his friends without changing one iota of his purpose.

Mr. Hines was not invited to Merrion, and the duke seemed pleased to give him the slip, if only for a few days, so that he departed from Castle Compton with a delight he had some trouble in concealing. The Arnotts received him with open arms, and their welcome was so genuine, that he could not for a moment entertain the suspicion that they hoped to make capital out of him in the way of arranging an alliance between him and the daughter, though it was known to all that he had been very fond of Emily before he went abroad.

When away from the companionship of Mr. Hines, and freed from that restraint which the tutor unquestionably exercised over him, his spirits expanded, and he appeared to greater advantage than at other times. He was merry and jovial; he talked openly, and was pronounced an agreeable companion. His stay at the Hall was made as pleasant for him as the hospitality of a good old country family could make it, and that is saying a great deal, for nowhere in the world can so much enjoyment be derived as in a country house in England.

'I wonder,' Masborough took an opportunity of observing to Captain Arnott, ' if your sister thinks of me as she did before I went away?'

' I have always heard her mention you with respect,' replied the captain.

' She is a dear girl,' the duke went on thoughtfully.

Wishing to turn the conversation, Captain Arnott said, ' So you think of training horses, and running them on the turf?'

' Who told you so?'

' I scarcely know. It may have been yourself. I heard it somewhere.'

' You heard the truth, anyhow,' said Masborough with a laugh; ' that is my intention. I was always passionately fond of horses, and a race has a peculiar excitement for me, which I can derive from nothing else.'

' It is impossible for me to offer any opinion, of course,' continued the captain, ' but I question whether it is an amusement from which a man in your position is likely to derive any profit or advantage.'

' As for profit, my dear fellow,' answered Masborough, ' I never thought of such a thing. I know racing is expensive, but if I can't afford to go in for a luxury of that sort, who can?'

Captain Arnott said nothing more, and they went in to dress for dinner. In the evening Emily, who was an accomplished musician, played and sung. She gave peculiar charms to ' Ah! che la morte!' and Masborough listened in an abstracted manner to the dying cadence of her voice.

' I hope my singing does not make you sad,' Miss Arnott said.

He started as if roused from a deep reverie, and answered, ' A little; I last heard that air of Verdi's at Venice.'

' Was the musician's voice so angelic as to impress it upon your memory?' continued Emily, toying with the keys, and not appearing to exhibit any curiosity.

' She was not an angel, she was a demon,' replied the duke, whose face clouded over fiercely.

' Byron tells us there is a land where all save the spirit of woman is divine,' said Emily. ' I should so like to hear the history of your demoniac songstress.'

' I trust you may never hear it, for it would only distress you. Please ask me no questions. You have called up memories I wished to bury for ever. Will you not kindly go on playing?'

' Pray excuse me, I am quite tired,' Miss Arnott rejoined, with slightly less amiability of manner.

' Thank you very much for the pleasure you have already afforded me,' said Masborough, as he closed the piano.

At this moment Mr. Arnott interrupted their languishing conversation by saying, ' I suppose you do not intend going abroad again, as your Grace has announced your intention of hunting the county and keeping racehorses?'

' No. I have had enough of the continent of Europe,' said the duke, ' and if I felt inclined to wander again, I think I should be tempted to run over to America.'

'The land that Dickens satirised in Pogram and Jefferson Brick, where, I have no doubt, a fund of amusement could be derived from that quarter.'

'At any rate I should not be away long. I have made up my mind to settle down here.'

'Marry and settle,' said the old gentleman, a little thoughtlessly.

'Perhaps,' said Masborough, venturing to look at Emily, who cast down her eyes and pretended to look for her pocket handkerchief.

'Marry!' said a voice at the door, 'who is talking of marriage? Pray pardon this unceremonious intrusion, Mrs. Arnott. I trust 1 may consider myself welcome. Mr. Arnott, good evening.'

The new arrival was Mr. Hines, who shook hands with every one, taking that of the duke last, who did not seem well pleased at being disturbed by his unexpected appearance.

'Make yourself at home, Mr. Hines,' said the master of the house, 'and do not apologise. You find us quite *en famille*, and I am sure we shall not find any excuse to you for being so.'

'You are too good,' answered Hines. 'My immediate object in coming was to inform his Grace that the duchess is not very well; bronchitis I am afraid, but nothing serious. Oh! dear no, nothing to be alarmed at. She merely expressed a wish to see our young friend in the morning. That is all. But, pray may I inquire who was talking of marrying? It is such an interesting subject, especially to young ladies, and I fear my unexpected appearance on the scene has interrupted some important announcement.'

'Not at all,' said Mr. Arnott. 'His Grace was talking of settling down.'

'Ah! yes. Very proper,' answered Mr. Hines, in his insinuating manner. 'But I will venture to say on his behalf, that he will not undertake such a responsible step for some time to come. Oh! no, perhaps not for years.'

'I don't think I should ask your opinion, Mr. Hines,' said Masborough, turning very pale.

'Possibly, no. Possibly, yes,' replied Hines with the utmost unconcern. 'Put me out of the question altogether. I am really nobody. If I speak about eventualities in which you may be concerned, I do so from a knowledge of your character, gained after long study. No, my dear fellow, depend upon it, you will not marry for some time to come.'

As he spoke he looked at Emily, and his dark eyes seemed to pierce her heart. She shuddered involuntarily as she encountered the man's glance, and he, perceiving the shiver run through her, smiled as if in subdued triumph.

He was invited to stay at the hall that night, and agreed to do so, as it was growing late. He knew that Mr. Arnott was fond of backgammon, and, accommodating himself to this taste, played several games with him, while the duke, Captain Arnott, and Emily, formed a little knot by themselves and talked.

'I am sorry you will have to leave us,' said the captain.

'It must be very annoying,' replied Emily, 'to have one's keeper always after one.'

'What do you mean, Miss Arnott?' asked the duke, flushing.

'Oh! Nothing. I alluded to your tutor, Mr. Hines. I used the wrong word, perhaps.'

'Indeed you did. Hines is not even my tutor now. He was my travelling companion, and very useful I found him. Now I employ him as my agent in various affairs.'

'Really I did not wish to go into an explanation of

your connection with Mr. Hines,' said Emily; 'you are too good-natured.'

'Upon my word,' began the duke.

'I am sorry the subject should be so disagreeable to you,' she interrupted. 'Cannot we talk about something else which you may find more interesting? I quite agree with my brother that it is extremely unfortunate you should be obliged to leave us so soon. I trust, though, sincerely that her Grace is not seriously ill.'

'I should not think so, from Hines's account,' answered Masborough, biting his lips.

His attitude to Mr. Hines was not improved during the evening by these remarks, for he was positively rude to him on more than one occasion, but Hines smiled in his usual way and appeared not to notice the slight.

When the duke returned for the night, he was followed into his bedroom by Hines, who lighted a cigar and sat down by the fire.

'Dreadfully slow in these country places,' he said, as the young nobleman leant with his back against the chimney-piece and looked at him. 'London is the place for you. In town you will be appreciated. You will take a position at once and a high one.'

'I am as ready and willing to commence the campaign as you are,' said the duke. 'What have you been doing?'

'Everything that I thought most conducive to your interests. You cannot expect to pull off any very big thing this year, although I have bought you a few horses entered for some of the great races, in order to bring your name prominently before the racing public. I have written a letter to the *Sporting Telegraph* in your name.'

'About what?'

'Weights in handicaps. It refers to the races at Newbridge, and will make you known in Ireland.'

Mr. Hines drew a sporting paper from his pocket and gave it to Masborough, who read an underlined paragraph to which his attention was directed.

'At the Newbridge races on Monday we observed a memorial to obtain the signature of owners of horses who have run their animals in a handicap steeple-chase, value 100 sovs., since January 1, 1870, as to whether they would prefer 10st. or 9st. 6lb. should be the lowest standard for weights in handicaps, and wo hear that only two voted for the former scale, and over fifteen were in favour of the latter. Amongst the most strenuous supporters of this rule is the young Duke of Masborough, an ardent lover of the turf, who is we hear about to assume a prominent place in the racing world. We hail this accession to the ranks of the breeders and runners of horses with much pleasure, as it is a proof that our leading noblemen do not hold aloof from the turf, and no one can say that the national sport is on the decline, when a nobleman possessing 100,000*l*. a-year, so it is said, in addition to a great historical name, comes forward as its champion and disciple.'

'You are a long-headed fellow, Hines,' said the duke, smiling.

'I don't know about that, but I think you are safe in my hands.'

'I might go all over London and not find a better agent,' the duke exclaimed, getting gradually into a better humour.

'You have a horse entered for the Liverpool.'

'Have I? What is the name?'

'Ville d'Orsay, one of the French division. Look in the first column of the paper and read what they say of it.'

The duke read the following somewhat to his astonishment : —

' Ville d'Orsay is one of the nicest mares I ever saw, and a wonderfully clever steeplechaser. Last year she won the Grand National Hurdle Race at Croydon in a canter, beating a number of good horses, and she almost lost Marsyas in a steeplechase at Shrewsbury. At Warwick last autumn she won the Warwick steeple-chase after meeting with a mishap that would have lost the race to nine animals out of ten, and she fairly walked in for the Grand Metropolitan at Croydon. She was backed for money to-day, the price high, and the ardour of her friends does not appear to be cooling down. This mare has recently become the property of the Duke of Masborough, which is sufficient to induce the public to back it to any amount.'

' They seem to mention my name often enough,' said the duke : ' why is that ?'

' Shall I tell you ?' asked Mr. Hines.

' I wish you would. I am not good at riddles.'

' It is your paper.'

' Mine !'

' Yes. I have bought it, and the editor shall take his cue from me.'

' By Jove, you are a wonderful fellow, Hines !' the duke said, regarding him with undisguised admiration.

' Shall I tell you something else ?'

' As you like.'

' I have taken the liberty of having your house at Merton, in Lincolnshire, fitted up, and have sent out invitations in your name to the most influential members of the aristocracy.'

' For what purpose ?'

' To witness the sport at the Grand National and Merton Hunt Steeplechases.'

' I did not know there was such a race.'

' Nor I, until a few weeks ago, when I originated the fixture. The entries are excellent and numerous. It will be a splendid affair. I want you to start for Merton to-morrow to lend your presence to everything.'

' I have not been there since I was a boy. Does the paper say anything about it?'

' Our paper? Yes, of course.'

Mr. Hines pointed out another paragraph, which said—

' The Grand National and Merton Hunt, near Lincoln, on Tuesday and Wednesday, will be a very brilliant affair; and during the *réunion* the Duke of Masborough, *on dit*, will entertain the Prince of Wales and other distinguished visitors. The Grand National Hunt Steeplechase, on Tuesday, is a contest manifestly framed to offer encouragement to high-class hunters, and has a large entry. Among the nominations are Downshire, who was third in the Two Thousand, and who was formerly in the Fyfield stable, and supposed at one time to possess Derby form. The Duke of Masborough has a couple in Monastery and the Prince (not the Cesarewich hero), and the issue may be confined to the three specified. Downshire is also reported to be trained by the duke's own hunting groom, and, if the horse has been converted into a perfect jumper, he is certain to win. At all events, we shall rely on Downshire and one of his Grace's (Monastery or Prince). The Merton Handicap Power or Dormouse will win, and Greenback or Ptarmigan the Handicap Plate of 100*l.* The Lincolnshire Hunters' Plate Merrythought should secure. Wednesday will have for its main attraction the Lincoln Grand National Steeplechase, which, despite its 500*l.* added, has not a large entry. Sanctus will, perhaps, not be risked over this big country, but be reserved for the easier track of Croydon, or otherwise he would have the duke's own good word.'

'You don't let the grass grow under your feet,' observed the duke. 'I am like Byron, who went to bed obscure and woke to find himself famous.'

'You do not object at all?' asked Mr. Hines.

'Not in the least. I rather like it. If one is to do this sort of thing, the sooner a start is made the better.'

'I want you to make a book on all the races. If you have not forgotten my instructions at Baden, you will not find it difficult.'

'I have the theory perfectly. What are the Derby horses this year. That is the race to begin with, I suppose?' said Masborough.

'Consult the leader in the paper,' answered Hines.

The duke did so, and was informed.

'It is a notable fact that the winter has passed without disturbing the positions of the favourites for the Derby; and, indeed, Dinmont and Aristides are firmer than ever. Flaming reports are circulated as to the great improvement made by the Russley crack; and it is the steadfastly maintained opinion of his former trainer that the horse will win the double event—Two Thousand and Derby. Aristides has just gone through a course of physic, preparatory to putting him into long work for the Epsom struggle. It is believed to be his owner's determination to decline the Newmarket Biennial, and run the son of Storm King and Cloud for no engagement until the Derby. The Middle Park Plate hero, like his Russley rival, has made much improvement, and the common impression is that the Berkshire pair will finish first and second on the Surrey Downs. Sampson, if he goes on the right way, will split them, and it has always been my opinion that, barring Riddler, the scion of Ludovicus was, when well, the best two-year-old in training. *Apropos* of Riddler, intelligence from America states that Mr. Strut, a wealthy transatlantic turfite, has sent over a commissioner to offer 3000*l.* for this noted animal; but this is not likely to be accepted if the son of Balderson retains his form, and has made the ordinary progress. The two great cracks almost monopolise the Derby betting, and as the spring advances the prospects of an outsider's triumph appear to diminish.'

'I could not get your name in this,' remarked Hines, ' as you have no nomination in this year's Derby, although you will come in handsomely the year after next, and even next year you will have a chance, as I have bought a couple of promising two-year-old's for you. I should make a book on the Lincolnshire Handicap and the Chester Cup. They are most thought of at present.'

'I don't know that I shall always bother about making a book,' said the duke, with a yawn of anticipated weariness. 'I shall pick out a horse and back him, trusting to luck. That is easiest.'

'Very well; do that. See what we say about Lincoln.'

Again Masborough took up the paper and read—

'For the Lincolnshire Handicap 10 to 1 was offered on the field without a response, while Falkenstein, on the contrary, was in great request, opening at 100 to 8 and leaving off at a point less taken freely. Bolingbroke had a coming tendency, 500 to 30 having been booked in his favour, while Sisyphus also had friends who were unable to procure better terms. Sempronius was in better demand than hitherto, but, as bookmakers refused to make a fraction of advance upon 9 to 1, no business resulted. The Physician was nominally second favourite, but offers of 11 to 1 were disregarded, and, although at first twelve ponies was accepted about the Skeleton, he left off at 100 to 8 offered. Sunrise's position it was difficult to guess at for a length of time, but the acceptance of twenty ponies, and several lesser bets at the same rate of odds, afforded some clue to the tone of the market, especially as Surrey could not command a bid at the same price. A few trifling investments on Hyacinth at 20 to 1 were negotiated after vain attempts to get on at longer odds. The hostility to Gem was exchanged this afternoon for a general disposition to back him, 25 to 1 being taken whenever procurable, while, at the same time, 200 to 5 and 1000 to 30 were booked in well-informed quarters about his stable companion, Batrakos. Hunter was frequently inquired after, and anything over 25 to 1 would have brought him a fair amount of support. We heard Rogue mentioned by a certain influential commissioner, but without eliciting an offer. Elevation was backed to win a couple of thousand pounds at 40 to 1, but layers were not disposed to continue their operations at that price. The Chester Cup was very flat, nothing worthy of comment having been done thereon. The best offer on the field for the Guineas was 900 to 200, while Dinmont was backed for 100*l*. at 5 to 1, and a level hundred betted that he beats Jay. Only two transactions were recorded on the Derby.'

'I'll plunge on Falkenstein and trust to chance. If I lose it does not matter; one must buy one's experience,' said the duke.

'At all events, you see the time has come to be active. You could not draw back now if you wanted,' replied Hines.

'I have no inclination to do so.'

'Will you start for Merton Hall after seeing your mother to-morrow, and, when the races are over, go to Epsom and see the training quarters I have established there for you?'

'Yes; I leave it all to you. I am entirely in your hands; do the work as you have begun, let me have the pleasure and the fun of the thing.   I don't care so long as I'm not bothered,' replied the duke.

'I feel proud of your confidence, and now to bed. Good night.'

' Good night.'

They shook hands and Mr. Hines went away, feeling that his position was now thoroughly secure.

CHAPTER IV.

NICHOLAS COPER, TRAINER.

NICHOLAS COPER was a middle-aged man, born at New-market, who thoroughly understood the training and management of horses ; he had been engaged by Mr. Hines as the Duke of Masborough's trainer, and all the horses which he had purchased were taken to extensive premises at Epsom, which had been hired for the purpose of a large training establishment.

The antecedents of Mr. Coper were not such as to bear inspection ; he liked to have people in his power. It facilitated any business he might have with them. If he could put the screw on, they were docile and obedient when they might otherwise have asserted their independence.

A short time after the conversation recorded in the last chapter, Mr. Hines and the trainer were seated in a neatly furnished parlour in the latter's house, which adjoined the stables ; on a table stood sundry bottles, glasses, and a box of cigars.

' I think, Coper, you thoroughly understand me ? ' said Mr. Hines.

' Yes, sir,' answered Coper, ' I think I do.'

' I must have implicit obedience. If I say to you a horse is not to win, it must lose. The horses under your care belong to the Duke of Masborough, but you belong to me.'

The trainer winced.

' It matters very little,' pursued Mr. Hines, ' how I discovered three years ago you committed a robbery at

Newmarket, and disposed of the notes in London. The fact remains the same. You did it. You are no less a thief, Coper, because you have not been publicly exposed and punished.'

'I was drove to it,' said Coper, sullenly.

'Possibly; criminals generally have some excuse to urge in extenuation of their offence. You are no exception to the general rule, and if it is a salve to your conscience to think that you were compelled to break the laws of your native land, by all means continue to do so.'

'It's no use reminding me of what's past and gone,' said Coper, with the same dogged air, as he helped himself to some more brandy and water.

'Yes, it is of use,' persisted Mr. Hines, who rather enjoyed the way in which the man writhed before him. 'It's not past and gone as you observe. It is ever present to me and to you. If you do not obey me as if you were my slave, I shall make the fact of your having been a thief unpleasantly patent to you. I do not say this to hurt your feelings, but to make you thoroughly understand your position.'

'The duke's horses, sir, shall be run just as you order; will that do?'

'That is more reasonable; and mind, no resistance, no kicking over the traces. I am going in to make money, and by watching my game you may do the same.'

'Thank you kindly, sir.'

'I suppose you have seen a few strange things in your time, Coper?' pursued Hines, picking a cigar out of the box.

'Well, I may say a few, sir,' answered Coper with a quiet chuckle.

'Perhaps you are not indisposed to favour me with a little of your experience?'

'Not at all, sir. I've seen some strange rigs on the turf, and that's a fact. If you want villany that's naked, as we may say, you must go on a racecourse for it. I think the turf's done a great deal to elevate and reduce to a science, as it were sir, the crime of the country. I've seen drunkenness, embezzling, late hours, bad company, loss of situation, broken homes, broken hearts, property sold, gambling, fighting and murder, ay, even murder, all come of what people call attendance at race meetings, and it's my opinion that Government would have to shut up some of the prisons if there was no horse-racing. It may seem odd to hear such an opinion coming from me, for I'm not a sentimental or a moral sort of a cove at all, but if I can't bring a sound judgment to bear upon it, having been in it all my life, who can?'

'I can't agree with you,' answered Mr. Hines. 'The turf is an arena worthy of the attention of noblemen and gentlemen. It is a national pastime, and a little judicious wagering can do no one any harm.'

'That's it, sir. You can do it, oh! you're a deep 'un,' cried Mr. Coper, rubbing his hands and laughing as if at a great joke.

'Did not you train once for Mr. Deadsell?'

'Yes, and I can tell you how we got hold of some money over an event which did not look promising. The governor had a horse entered for a small race, called Grasshopper, and he was so good that no one would lay against him. I thought we had better scratch the horse as we could not get on at anything like a decent price—we were forestalled everywhere, but the governor did not like to put the pen through his name and put on his considering cap instead. The end of it was that he went to Mr. Bates, who is a sharp man and thinks he knows a thing or two. He says to Bates, that he was hard up and wanted a couple of

thousand.   Bates asks him for the security, not liking
personal security, and Deadsell offers him the horse.

' " Grasshopper is a good animal and can win the Cup
if he likes," he says, " and I'll mortgage him to you."

' " Sell him outright," says Bates.

' " No ; I won't do that.   I'll mortgage him to you,
and if the money is not repaid he shall be your property
within a given time."

' " Say three months," suggests Bates.

' " No.   Put it like this.   If I do not give you the
money anytime on the morning of the race or before it,
the horse is yours.   If I do, though the bell may be
ringing to clear the course at the time, the horse is mine."

' " All right," says Bates, and Deadsell goes away
with a cheque in his pocket.

' Deadsell did not want the money, you know, sir,
though he kidded Bates he did, and Bates thinking he'd
never be able to redeem the animal, and that his hopes
was to win money by backing the horse, and that he
wanted the coin to put on, made up his mind to lay
against the horse everywhere, and pull him.   Accordingly he got his own jockey and gave him instructions
how to ride, while he put out commissions everywhere
to bet against Grasshopper, and wherever there was
any money to be had, Deadsell took him.   By this
means we got on a very tidy sum.   We knew what
Bates' game was, but he did not know ours, no, not so
much as a ha'p'oth even.   When the day of the race
came the two met on the course.

' " How do? " says Bates.   " Want to back your
horse ?"

' " Don't mind for a thou., take you to a thou.," replies
Deadsell.

' " Done, with you.   Who's the next ?"

' " Stop a minute, I've some money for you," Deadsell
exclaims.

' " What for ? "

' " The horse. I want him back again. Here are twenty, hundred pound notes; take them, and here's our agreement."

' Bates turned white, and said—

' " After the race will do, don't be in a hurry."

' " Now, I say; I want my horse," Deadsell continued.

' When Bates saw the game was up, he grew frantic; he couldn't help giving the horse up, you know, and we at once took possession of him. I stood over him, till the jock mounted, and kept a loaded pistol in my hand. Well, Bates wired to all parts of the country to try and hedge, but it was no go. We ran the horse square and won easy. That caper nearly bust Mr. Bates up, it did, and he's never been the same since. If you want to rile him, ask him if he'll advance anything on equine security; he'll go mad, horseflesh ain't good enough for him, oh, no ; not by a long way.'

Mr. Hines laughed, and in listening to the trainer's experience the afternoon passed; he then returned to town, going first to his office in Jermyn Street. He called himself a financial agent, which is a term to cover any swindling transaction a man chooses to embark in, just as every man of straw, who turns builder and fails, calls himself in his petition to the Court of Bankruptcy, C.E., as if he were a civil engineer, because he had erected half a dozen brick monstrosities in the suburbs, with other peoples' money, which he is pleased, in the extravagance of his imagination, to designate villas.

MR. S. HINES,

Financial Agent.

looked well on a brass plate, and he rather flattered

himself upon the ingenuity of the idea. Financial agent was deliciously vague; he might be a money lender, or the promoter of a company for the irrigation of the Great Sahara, or the levelling of the Carpathian mountains.

As he passed through the outer office he saw two people waiting for him, but taking no notice of them, he walked quickly into his own room, opened some letters which lay upon his desk, and then struck a call bell sharply.

His clerk entered.

' Who is waiting?' he asked.

' Mr. Overset, of the *Sporting Telegraph,* sir, and Mr. Pimplepeck,' replied the clerk.

' Show Mr. Overset in.'

A portly gentleman, who had for some years been connected with the press, and who was haughty enough to his inferiors, entered the room hat in hand, and bowing politely as a tribute of respect to so important a personage as the agent of the rich Duke of Masborough.

' Well, Overset, what is it?' cried Mr. Hine; ' I'm busy, and you must not keep me to-night.'

' I have brought a proof of the account of the meeting at Merton, sir, thinking you would like to see it before we go to press. If you will glance your eye over it, sir, I will wait, as we go on the machine at ten to-night,' answered the editor.

Hines took the slip and read it over carefully.

It was headed, ' Merton Hall Steeple-chase, by our Special Reporter,' and began, ' We are indeed fortunate in being able to chronicle such sport and such an attendance as has seldom distinguished a country meeting of late years. No one can fail to see that in the Duke of Masborough a nobleman has risen up amongst us who is determined to regenerate the turf, and place it on a high level, which will silence the voice of all carping cavillers.'

' Don't like that,' said Hines, pointing with his pen to the passage.

' What, sir ? Carping cavillers ? Fine line, sir.'

' Alter it.'

' Say—of all those who predict its fall in public esteem ?'

' That will do.'

' Public esteem—right, sir,' said the editor, making the necessary correction. The article went on. ' With such a name, with such a fortune, and with such truly national tastes, the Duke of Masborough cannot help being in an incredibly short space of time the most popular man in the country, nor will he by encouraging the breeding of horses be a slight benefactor to the land. A brilliant gathering of the aristocracy collected at Merton on Tuesday, and we do not recollect having seen so much beauty and so many well-known stars in the world of fashion for a long space of time. The urbanity of his Grace was observed by every one, and the irresistible charms of his manner admitted by both ladies and gentlemen.

' A large attendance of professionals and the outside public testified still further to the popularity of the Merton Hall Meeting, and the attraction that steeple-chasing has for pleasure-seekers. The weather being delightfully fine, the sport was enjoyed under the most satisfactory circumstances, and every one appeared delighted at the successful manner in which the meeting had been carried out. The card contained six races, and at a quarter-past one proceedings commenced with a Selling Handicap Hurdle Race, Pillory and Oberon being the two absentees from the seven animals entered. Miss Fanny was installed favourite from the commencement of the betting, and she left off in strong demand at 5 to 4. Chatterbox, notwithstanding her easy defeat recently by Stone, found plenty of friends willing to invest on her chance at 2 to 1. Neither Earl nor West-haven was fancied, and the last-named after landing over the hurdle at the stand broke down so badly that his jockey at once dismounted. The Earl and Chatter-box raced away side by side in advance of the others till within half-a-mile of home, where the last-mentioned was beaten, her display harmonising only with the feelings of those who had laid against her. The favourite then took the lead and appeared to be winning in a canter, but Astrologer came on hand over hand, and taking the lead at the distance, won in a common canter by four lengths. He was entered to be sold for 50 sovs., but there was no bid for him.

' Astrologer being the property of the Duke of Mas-borough, his victory was very popular with the crowd, and his triumph is considered a good omen for the new stable.

' The Open Handicap Steeple-chase came next, and being the most important event of the meeting it was regarded with considerable interest. Although there were twenty animals coloured on the card, but five put in an appearance, his Grace, who had three entered, being represented by Wishing Cap. Oat-straw was the top-weight of the handicap, but his absence created no surprise, notwithstanding the reports that had been circulated to the effect that he would be sent to the post. Elk arrived on Monday to fulfil his engagement, but his owner disposed of him on the following day to Lord Charles Ibbetson; the price did not transpire. Although Wishing Cap was penalised 10lb., raising his weight to 12st. 6lb., his admirers were confident in his ability to carry the crushing impost successfully, and he accordingly started a hot favourite at 5 to 4. Brewer, however, had a strong body of friends who backed him very freely, and after all the money had been absorbed at 4 to 1, a point less was accepted about his chance.

Old Acres was in great demand also, being backed for
a good stake down to 4 to 1. Flyer was not at all
fancied, but 100 to 8 was several times accepted about
Tomahawk. For the first mile and a half of the journey
the pace was wretchedly bad. Brewer, who had been
making the running, increased the speed considerably,
and the last time round it was noticed that its rider
had to bustle the favourite along to make him go the
pace. Half a mile from home he closed up, and for a
hundred yards it appeared as if he could overhaul the
leader, but, succumbing under the heavy weight, he
was unable to maintain his place. The Brewer, full of
running, increased his lead after clearing the last fence,
and won in a canter by half a dozen lengths from Flyer.
The contest was remarkable for the few changes that
occurred in the respective positions of the competitors,
who ran from end to end almost as they finished. The
winner used to be trained at Newmarket, and was at
one time looked upon as likely to be a " good thing." He
was greatly fancied to-day by many good judges on the
form he displayed at Croydon last November, when he
gave 16lb. to Chamberlain and beat him easily for the
Hunters' Stakes. The Merton Steeple-chase brought
out four runners from the half-dozen entered, and
although Temperance was meeting the Gardiner on
11lb. worse terms, her victory over him lately was
considered to have been gained so easily that her admirers laid odds of 11 to 10 on her. The Gardiner was
backed freely at 5 to 2, and as " weight will tell," he
was enabled to turn the tables on his conqueror of the
preceding day. The Hurdle Race Handicap resulted
in the easy victory of Spring over his stable companion,
Regulus, both of whom were very heavily backed.
Money, however, started favourite at 2 to 1, but she
could perform no better than last year; indeed, she
could only get third. Simpleton at one time was freely

backed, particularly at the " lists," at 5 to 1, but he was not fancied at the finish; indeed, 100 to 8 " bar three " was freely offered. For the two-miles Steeple-chase Plate half-a-dozen animals contended, and Alice, Hartshill, and Blessington were in such request that it was difficult to say which was favourite. At the close, however, Alice just had the call at 2 to 1, and she justified this confidence by winning in a canter; indeed, any odds were offered on her when more than half-a-mile from home. Hartshill, however, would have been a thorn in her side had she not fallen, but although Mr. Stoney Hines, her owner, who rode her in the most plucky manner, eliciting universal applause, remounted immediately, he could never make up the lost ground. The Maiden Steeple-chase Plate brought out a capital field, there being no fewer than ten runners from the seventeen animals entered. Egyptian was made a very hot favourite at 7 to 4, but Pyramus, whom many shrewd judges supported at 4 to 1, won in a canter by half-a-dozen lengths, the race, however, being well contested until within a quarter of a mile of the finish. There were a few bets laid on the Grand National during the afternoon, and the Lincoln Handicap was mentioned. Several members of the aristocracy are staying at the Hall, and many others were regaled at luncheon by his Grace, who fully sustained the character of the Dukes of Masborough for hospitality. Altogether we have had to chronicle a most enjoyable and successful day's sport.'

' Rather long, but it will do,' said Mr. Hines, handing the proof back to the editor.

' Any further instructions, sir?' inquired Mr. Overset.

' Not now; let me see you on Saturday.'

The editor bowed again and took his departure. Again the bell sounded, and Mr. Pimplepeck was ordered to come in, which he did in a somewhat nervous manner. He was a youth of anything but ingenuous appearance, for there was a sly look about his restless eyes. He had an unpleasant way of paying constant attention to a mole on his neck, which he was perpetually picking and irritating till it got into a state of inflammation terrible to contemplate. He was tall and thin, neatly dressed, and chiefly remarkable for a shiny hat, and boots very much down at heel.

' You are the gentleman who advertised for a situation, and to whom I wrote, I presume?' said Mr. Hines.

' Yes, as secretary to a nobleman or gentleman,' answered Mr. Pimplepeck, quoting from his advertisement.

' What are your qualifications?'

' I am a B.A., London.'

' Have you done anything disgraceful?' asked Mr. Hines.

' Sir!' cried Mr. Pimplepeck, working away at his mole with more energy than ever.

' Have you done anything disgraceful?' repeated Mr. Hines.

' Do you wish to insult me, sir?'

' I will put it another way. Should you have any objection to do anything disgraceful if you were paid for it. Let us understand one another,' said Mr. Hines, employing his favourite phrase.

' Not if I was paid for it,' replied Mr. Pimplepeck, leaving his mole alone for a moment in his astonishment at this peculiar mode of address.

' That is what I wanted to know. If I engage you for a nobleman, who is a friend of mine and wants a secretary, you will have to play the spy upon him ; to be my paid spy, in fact. I must have copies of all his private correspondence, and you must tell me everything that comes under your notice which you may think will interest me. You will have to worm yourself into his confidence in order to betray him, and do dirty work generally.'

' For which——'

' You will be paid three hundred a year, and can have the first quarter in advance. Remember one thing, though ; if I catch you at any double dealing, and find that you are not my slave in fact and in deed, you will be instantly dismissed. I am a dangerous man to trifle with, Mr. Pimplepeck.'

Mr. Pimplepeck thought so too, and worked away at his mole again.

' Well!' ejaculated Mr. Hines.

' I accept the situation, sir,' said Mr. Pimplepeck.

' On my terms?'

' On your terms.'

' Very well, call on me the day after to-morrow, at nine. I like early men, Mr. Pimplepeck.'

' So do I, sir. Expect to see me. Good evening.'

And Mr. Pimplepeck, who was a man of business, took his leave.

' Now I think everything is complete, and my lord duke may start along the road to ruin as soon as is agreeable to him,' soliloquised Mr. Hines.

He was indeed a clever fellow, and knew how to spread his net for an unsuspecting and foolish victim as well as any scoundrel who has ever flourished for a time on his ill-gotten gains.

CHAPTER V.

Mr. PIMPLEPECK occupied chambers in New Inn, and thither he repaired after his interview with Mr. Hines. His laundress had prepared tea for him, and he lighted a pipe and sat down in his arm-chair to reflect upon his good fortune.

'It matters very little to me what I do so long as I get the money,' he muttered. 'What use has my education been to me? I can write and manage to subsist by my pen, but what a subsistence it has been after all! Far better be a backwoodsman in the States, or an iron-puddler in Staffordshire. I can't afford to be scrupulous, and if Mr. Hines pays me, I will serve him as long as it suits me.'

There was a knock at the door. He rose and admitted Mr. Overset, who was a friend of his, and had looked in to know how he had succeeded with Mr. Hines. On hearing the result of his interview he congratulated him.

'I was about to offer you a berth as my sub-editor,' said Mr. Overset, 'but it is no use now.'

'These things always come when one doesn't want them,' remarked Mr. Pimplepeck a little bitterly, as he attacked his mole.

'I never was so worried with a staff in my life,' continued Mr. Overset. 'My sub. has got D. T., and fancies himself a steam-engine. He swings his arms about till he gets up the steam, and then he rushes at any one or anything that happens to be in his way. He insulted our special sporting commissioner to-day, by calling him an inflated tout and charging him full butt, hitting him in the stomach and quite knocking him out of time, as the special is rather stout, and cannot stand a fly on his waistcoat. We got him off home at last, but he'll break out, and I should not be surprised if he came down in the middle of the night and steam-engined into the composing room and upset all the formes. Our advertising agent's not much better. The last I had settled us, and this is a new man I put on last week.'

'I saw him at your office last week, I think; a tall man, with an extensive tawny beard, and a rather pompous manner. Pink and white in the face like a Madame Tussaud's waxwork.'

'That's the fellow. Read this letter I have just received from him; pleasant, isn't it, when advertisements are the backbone of the paper?'

'It's the duke's paper though, isn't it, and he doesn't care whether it pays or not?' said Mr. Pimplepeck.

'Mum as to that,' answered Mr. Overset cautiously. 'At all events, one is expected to do one's best for one's employers.'

'I suppose Mr. Hines has engaged me for the duke?'

'Most likely. You will know the day after to-morrow, and if so, we shall both be in the same swim.'

Mr. Pimplepeck took the letter offered him and read :—

'SIR,

'It is now some days since you did me the honour to appoint me one of your agents for procuring advertisements. I have commenced my canvass; it is an honourable occupation. I like it much. Thursday saw the conclusion of our agreement. I come of a diligent family, but I like to start on a Monday; this

the first day of the week looks well; during the in-
tervening time I matured my plans. I was not idle,
far from it. I looked over the papers and made a list
of names of those I thought likely to go into the
" S.T." My adventures have been startling. I have
not pulled off anything yet, but I have several big
orders in hand. One for a very large amount will
astonish you, but I am not at liberty to speak fully
at present. On Monday I got up early and left my
home—my address is 8, Carthusian Buildings, Charter-
house Square, E.C. I like being central—under my
arm was a bundle of *Sporting Telegraphs*. My first
point was a great mourning emporium in Regent Street.
With a bounding heart I crossed the Viaduct—splendid
work of art the Viaduct, but rather suggestive in its
surroundings of Strasburg after the bombardment.
When I reached the emporium, I entered fearlessly;
my attire and general appearance induced the young
gentleman behind the counter to regard me as a
customer. I flatter myself my get-up is faultless,
sealskin vest, this style, 17s. 6d., Sydenham trousers,
great coat trimmed with Astrachan fur, dog-skin
gloves, small cane, Gibus hat. Good thing, a Gibus
hat, will stand the rain. In reply to a question as to
what I might please to want this morning, I intimated
a wish to see the proprietor. The great man was sitting
at a desk in a corner. I am afraid his eggs and bacon
had not agreed with him that morning, he looked
bilious, and he was cross; he demanded my business as
I approached him. In an insinuating tone I told him
that I came on a little matter of advertising. " Call
again in a month," he replied, " we are not spending
money now. What's your paper?" " The *Sporting Telegraph*," said I. " Hum!" said he, as if he had never
heard of it. Benighted being! " It's no use now,
look in again," he continued. Determined not to be

abashed, I exclaimed, " Allow me, sir, to parade before you the advantages which this periodical beyond all others offers. The circulation is over half a million, and the King of Prussia has ordered fifty quires for distribution among the troops before Paris. We penetrate the palace, and we do not disdain the cottage. The toil of the labourer is soothed by the perusal of our pages, and the haughty aristocrat melts into a smile," when I stopped suddenly, for the great man had vanished through a side door, and I had only an audience of tittering assistants. However, his explanation was perfectly satisfactory, he was not spending money, so I thought it was best to wend my way, and I wended. The next on my list was a wine merchant. I like wine merchants. One gave me a tasting order for the docks years ago. The fumes of the wine got into my legs. I went home in a cab ; but this is a digression. The establishment was called the " Losaga," I do not know why. Perhaps it is Spanish for something nice. There were casks all round the place. There was a bar in the centre, and barmaids. Pretty girls as a rule, barmaids ; I like them much. It was my intention only to stay a few minutes. I had a long list of names to collect. I considered myself in treaty with the proprietor of the mourning emporium, as he had asked me to call again. It is a good thing to be in treaty with a large house. I could not spare much time, I belong to a diligent family, and I am full of work. Sherry is tempting, especially when dry. I was dry, and would try some. Just a glass. It is not my custom to imbibe before ten in the morning, but it was close upon that hour. I imbibed. The sherry was good ; I imbibed again, feeling that my courage required stimulating. I was new to the business. I am deficient in impudence ; it is my only failing. I inquired for the proprietor, and hoped that he was spending money, or if he was not, I was. He was out, but the manager was in; he was pointed out to me, a tall, thin man, sitting on a cask. With a bow I informed him that I represented a newspaper of vast influence. He was happy to be informed of the fact. Would he go in? He thought I meant, would he take a drink, and he ordered an old port. I did not like to hang back, so I also ordered an old port. Very nice place, the "Losaga," they sell good stuff. He drank, he looked at my paper, our paper, and he laughed. I thought this a good sign. " What is your sale price?" said he. I informed him. " Very good medium, I should think," said he. " Excellent!" I answered, " finest in the world; take half a page?" "Well, I don't mind if I do," he said, and he handed his glass to the nearest barmaiden. He mistook my meaning; no matter, I paid. Very nice place, the "Losaga." Port especially commendable, though rather heavy at ten in the morning. Bitter is more my form. The manager at length said he could do nothing without the proprietor, would I wait; he would be in about one. I waited. We had more drinks. I paid for them. At twelve o'clock I came to the conclusion that the manager was a most incarnate sponge, he absorbed. However we were good friends. He said it would be all right; I felt all wrong. At one o'clock I saw two managers and the pretty barmaids were multiplied in my eyes. I tore myself away, but I am in treaty with the "Losaga." Nice place, the "Losaga," but rather insinuating. I concluded not to do any more work that day, so went home in a cab, to think over to-morrow's campaign. You shall have full particulars. My landlady opened the door to me as I could not find my key. In the evening I had some tea. I feel that I shall do a great deal of business for you, as I come of a diligent family, and know how to represent things. I have great confidence in the future; we shall do big things together, as I mean business. I beg to subscribe myself your faithful canvasser.'

'I should call him a very valuable man to have on the staff, and decorate him with the universal Order of the Sack and Bullet,' remarked Mr. Pimplepeck.

'I shall at once, never fear,' replied Mr. Overset, who, looking round him, saw some sheets of paper recently covered.

'Something new?' he added; 'may I look?'

'If you like,' answered Pimplepeck, filling his pipe. 'It's not much. I sent the tale to a magazine, and the editor with that charming liberality which distinguishes his class sent it back again. Perhaps he was right. Perhaps it wasn't worth printing. At all events I have turned it to account by altering the finish so as to suit the enterprising firm of Clapper and Treadle, the sewing-machine makers, who are going to use it as a bill. It may be a degradation of the author's art, but one must keep the pot boiling, and after all, to raise the standard of advertisers' English is doing good to the community at large. I think I am entitled to credit for such an ingenious idea. Read it and tell me what you think of it. There isn't much of it. First you have the straightened circumstances at home, *res angusta domi* you know; then emigration, then the wreck, then the savages, and finally the puff insidious.

Mr. Overset cast his eyes over the MS. and read—

Times were bad in England.

James Hudson was a dockyard hand, and when the ministers of the Crown thought it advisable to reduce the establishments of the country, he with others was discharged. Now a shipwright is not a man who can easily find employment.

He thought of going to the banks of the Clyde, but

learnt that the yards there were over-crowded. Ship-building on the Thames was in a state of stagnation. So James Hudson remained at Woolwich, with the gaunt spectre of coming starvation staring him in the face.

He could not adopt Earl Russell's motto, ' Rest, and be thankful.'

To be up and doing was his wish. Activity was his sphere.

It *was* hard to see his household goods going one by one to the pawnbrokers for that daily bread which, through no fault of his own, he was debarred from earning.

At last, in sheer desperation, he bethought him of the Emigration Commissioners, and made an application to be sent out somewhere. He was successful. Dearly as he loved his country, he preferred expatriation to the workhouse, and determined to leave his native land.

His wife said she would go anywhere with him. They had no children, so they sold what furniture remained to them, and quickly make their preparations.

Australia was the colony to which he was to be sent, and though he had no clear idea of what he would do when he got there, he was ready to turn his hand to anything and everything.

The good ship, ' Golden Star,' sailed in the autumn from the London Docks, with several emigrants and a large cargo.

She made a prosperous voyage until she had performed two-thirds or thereabouts of the journey, when a storm arose which disabled the ship.

The vessel drifted towards the land, which was said by the officers to be inhabited by savages.

Some took to the boats and were never heard of more; others remained on board till the ' Golden Star' drove on the rocks and became a total wreck.

E

Hudson and his wife clung to a spar, and, praying to heaven for protection and deliverance, were washed ashore.

They of all the ship's company and passengers were the only ones fortunate enough to reach the land.

Almost immediately they were surrounded by savages, half naked, and of a ferocious aspect, who by signs gave them to understand that they were prisoners.

A party escorted them inland to a town composed of rudely-constructed huts, and after allowing them some food, consisting of the flesh of wild animals and rice, compelled them to work in various menial occupations.

The unhappy captives saw that they were doomed to a life of slavery, and their tears fell fast.

Other of the natives proceeded in canoes to the wreck, as soon as the violence of the storm had moderated, and brought to shore such of the cargo as they were able to save.

They obtained in this way a large quantity of calico and cotton prints in pieces, some of which they tore up, and fantastically arrayed their bodies in.

' If I only had a needle and cotton,' said Mrs. Hudson when she saw that, ' I might make clothes for the poor creatures.'

But such things as needles and cotton had never been seen in the country since human beings existed on it.

A few days afterwards they saw the chief standing in perplexity before something, which excited his liveliest curiosity.

He beckoned to James to approach.

' Why, I never,' cried Mrs. Hudson, ' if he hasn't got a sewing machine ! I remember there was a consignment of Clapper and Treadle's silent machines on board the " Golden Star." '

She was right.

The natives had obtained from the wreck a handsome sewing machine, manufactured by those celebrated makers, and with it a box of cottons, needles, and everything requisite for its proper working for a long period of time.

Calling his wife, who thoroughly understood its management, James stood by, while the delighted natives saw her cut up a piece of cotton printing, and make a dress for the chief's wife.

This lady was charmed with her new attire.

All the females adopted the new fashion of wearing something, and Mrs. Hudson was kept in constant employment.

Instead of being treated as slaves, the captives were given a house to live in, and paid great attention. They had servants assigned them, and were supplied with as good provisions as graced the table of the chief.

When the females were clothed the men came in for their share of the other stuffs, and soon presented the appearance of a civilised community.

Six months passed, and at the end of that time a sailing vessel, driven by stress of weather, cast anchor near the shore.

James Hudson communicated with them by signal.

The captain of the ship sent a boat to shore, and made arrangements to take the captives on board with him.

Very sorry were the natives to part with them. Each brought a present of ivory or gold dust, until James found himself the possessor of a large treasure.

He bid his kind friends adieu with genuine regret, and sailed to Sydney, whither the ship was bound, and there sold his ivory and gold dust for a good round sum, which enabled him to start in business.

Now he is a rich merchant, and has many ships of his own.

In all their prosperity the husband and wife never

E 2

forgot that they owed their success to the accidental use of one of Clapper and Treadle's silent sewing machines.

We may add, *par parenthèse*, that many others, in a different way, owe their success in life to the same indispensable article of domestic use.

But this by the way.

'Very neatly put,' answered Mr. Overset, when he had finished.

'Isn't it?' said Mr. Pimplepeck, much delighted. 'There is a free and easiness about my style which would, I flatter myself, render me particularly useful to the sporting aristocracy among whom I am about to move. I will adapt myself to the stable and write slang as they talk it, and—'

'What's more to the purpose, if you hear what is going on in the stable let me know,' interrupted Mr. Overset; 'Mr. Hines only tells me what he likes, and if I could get any direct information from you, all the better for both of us. I shall know how to turn it to account.'

'Rely upon me. My opinion of Mr. Hines is this. He is one of those men who will either land himself the owner of ten thousand a year in somebody else's ancestral domains, or in Newgate.'

'That's no business of ours.'

'Not in the least. I'll drink his health.'

'So will I.'

Mr. Pimplepeck and Mr. Overset being quite in accord, shook hands and fraternised exceedingly. The former was so much pleased with the prospect before him that he led his mole a very hard life of it for the next two minutes, and when he left off his delicate attention, it glowed like a fiery coal.

We have now given a brief account of Mr. Nicholas Coper, Mr. Overset, and Mr. Pimplepeck, trainer, editor, and secretary. Such were the tools Mr. Hines had chosen to work with.

Meanwhile the time passed on.

The Duke of Masborough became as notorious as ever he could wish, and his name was continually in everybody's mouth for some wild escapade or other. Mr. Hines ran his horses as he pleased and made money, while the duke, it need scarcely be said, lost it.

As an instance of how he was made use of by indifferent scoundrels, we will relate an anecdote of what befel him in one of those nocturnal resorts where night birds and scamps congregate to drink bad champagne, and think that they are leading a fast life and doing the proper thing.

The duke was sitting upon a luxuriously cushioned divan. The room was crowded. The time half-past twelve. He had a friend by his side. The gas was glaring, also champagne flowing. A betting man of the lowest order and a professed pugilist dropped his hat in front of the duke and said in an insolent tone,—

'Masborough, pick up my hat!'

The duke's blood rushed to his face, and rising indignantly he trod on the hat, crushing it out of shape. That done, he resumed his seat. It being the eve of the Ascot Cup the place was crowded, and the people present looked forward with pleasant anticipation to a row.

'Your Grace has insulted me!' said the betting-man, whose name was Clincher, 'and if you don't want me to punch your head here, you will come into an inner room and fight me for fifty pounds a side. You're man enough for that, I suppose.'

The proprietor of the establishment, who, it may be mentioned, was in this little piece of business, came up, it having been arranged between him and Clincher a few minutes previously. His name was Tarpot.

'Better do as he says, my lord,' said Mr. Tarpot; 'you can lick him easy. He can't fight. He's a bully. A gentleman can always welt a rough.   Give him what he deserves, I'll see fair play.   You can have my kitchen for a dust up.'

'Very well,' answered the duke, whose blood was on fire.

They went downstairs to the kitchen, and the table being pushed on one side, they took off their coats and stood opposite each other.

'Fifty pounds a side,' said Clincher; 'that's understood, isn't it?'

'Yes, that's all right; you needn't be in a hurry to part,' replied Tarpot on behalf of the duke.

They then set to, and Clincher contented himself with hitting the duke continually on the nose, until that unoffending member began to swell up in a most alarming manner.

After the tenth round, Mr. Tarpot held up a looking-glass before Masborough, saying, 'You've copt it on the nose, my lord; it's a swelling awful, and to-morrow, the cup day, you'll never be fit to be seen.'

'I must go,' replied Masborough.

'You can't, my lord, if your beauty's spylt,' returned Tarpot.

'I can lick that ruffian; I feel sure of it. I'm as fresh as ever, and he has two black eyes already.'

'Well, if you like to go to Ascot with a nose as big as a saveloy, my lord, it's no business of mine. I only thought I'd tell you.'

'Devil take the fellow, I suppose I must let him off. Give me my coat and a pen and ink; I'll write him a cheque for fifty.'

He did so, and handing it to Mr. Clincher, said, 'Here you are; I give it you because I am not a blackguard, and must turn out to-morrow. If it had not been for that I'd have pounded your ugly face into a jelly for you.'

' Your Grace has paid forfeit,' said Clincher, with a grin, ' and it don't much matter what you say now.'

' Tarpot !' exclaimed the duke, ' I insist upon that fellow being instantly turned out, and give me some hot water.'

' Take care of the proboscis, my lord,' cried Clincher, as he went up the stairs. The duke threw the water jug at him, but missed his aim. He bathed his nose, and was soon upstairs again, little dreaming that the whole affair had been arranged to get fifty pounds out of him, and that he was purposely only hit on the nose to disfigure it, and to make him leave off the contest. But so it was, and an hour afterwards Mr. Tarpot and Mr. Clincher with mutual satisfaction divided the plunder.

Kempson, the Duke's valet, obtained some powder of a miraculous nature, which was supposed to be an antidote to bruises, and applied it to the injured part, on his Grace's return to his house in Hill Street, Berkeley Square.

This man was an old servant of the Masboroughs, and had the greatest possible love and respect for his master.

On leaving Compton Castle, the duchess had taken him on one side, saying, ' Kempson, you are a trustworthy fellow.'

' I hope so, your Grace,' he replied.

' You will have a great insight to my son's private life, because you will be always with him. Now I want you to promise me you will look after him, and put him on his guard if you see any plot being hatched for his ruin.'

' I'll do my best,' Kempson said.

' You will promise me this, Kempson ? '

' On the word of a man, your grace.'

The duchess was satisfied, and Kempson felt the pride of one in whom confidence was placed.

Being a shrewd, keen fellow, he quickly saw that Mr. Hines had surrounded his master with his own creatures, and he kept a particular watch upon Mr. Pimplepeck, for whom he had a strong aversion.

This evening he exclaimed, as he was arranging the duke's slippers and dressing-gown for the morning after his Grace had got into bed, flushed with wine and excitement—

' You'll excuse me, I hope, your Grace, if I unburden my mind a bit ? '

' Give me a soda and B. first, my good fellow, and I'll listen to you,' answered Masborough.

Kempson did so, and went on. ' I am afraid Mr. Hines is not altogether square.'

' How's that ? '

' He thinks of feathering his own nest, and Pimplepeck's only a spy.'

' In what way ?   What makes you say that ? ' asked the duke.

' Because he often goes to Mr. Hines in the evening when he leaves here, and gives him notes of what you've said and done, and ordered him to write.   You had better be on your guard ; if not, your Grace may find out these men too late.'

' Nonsense, Kempson ; you bore me.'

' It is not nonsense,' replied Kempson, doggedly.

' Tell me to-morrow ; I shan't sleep if I'm bothered,' said the duke.

' Very well ; I've done my duty in warning your Grace, and if you won't listen to me it's not my fault.'

' Be off, and call me early for Ascot,' cried the duke, turning over to go to sleep.

With a sigh Kempson put out the lights, and went away.

On the stairs he muttered—' I promised her Grace I'd look after him, and I'll keep my word. He's got a pack of scoundrels about him who are bent on eating him up, and if that Hines is not a precious villain, I'll never touch a glass of beer again. Yes, I'll do my best, and please God I'll save him yet.'

Thus in the person of this poor man-servant did a mother's love show itself, and he watched over him in his folly, though he was far from giving him credit for his affection, nor did he really know what a kind, generous heart beat under the rough exterior of so apparently an insignificant person as Kempson.

CHAPTER VI.

AFTER TWO YEARS.

A GREAT deal may be done in two years in dissipating a large fortune, and in the Duke of Masborough's case a great deal was done.

The duke lost prodigious sums of money, and Mr. Hines, as a matter of course, reaped the benefit of his folly.

But it happened that certain events occurred for which Mr. Hines was unprepared, and they eventually upset all his calculations.

It may be readily imagined that her son's folly caused the duchess infinite annoyance

In vain she remonstrated with him, and Mr. Whittaker was equally unsuccessful in his good-natured efforts to stop his foolish career.

In the midst of his dissipation and folly, it was evident that Masborough was not happy. He was restless and uneasy. The obedience which he yielded to Hines galled him, and his recklessness was that of a species of despair.

One day the duchess, accompanied by Mr. Whittaker, called upon the duke at his chambers in St. James's. It was early in the morning, but his Grace was astir, and his drag stood at the door. A great race in the neighbourhood of London was to be run that day, and he had promised to drive a select circle of friends to the meeting.

He was glad to see his mother, so he said, and felt honoured by Mr. Whittaker's visit, but he begged that they would excuse him, as he had an important engagement.

' I cannot excuse you, Arthur,' replied his mother; ' because I have come on business of a much more important nature than can possibly take up your time.'

' The old, old story, I suppose,' the duke said, with a yawn. ' Prodigal son, and all that sort of thing.'

' Not exactly,' replied the duchess; ' I have come to save you.'

' From what ? '

' The destruction with which you are threatened, and to release you.'

' Once more, what from ? '

' The thraldom of Mr. Hines—your evil genius.'

' But I do not admit that there is any thraldom,' said Masborough, uneasily.

' My dear Arthur, whatever you do and say in the world, you must not trifle with your mother. You are in that bad man's power, and you cannot deny it.'

' Well, what have you to say about it? I will not contradict you,' he remarked, after a pause.

' I know all about his hold over you, and I can free you.'

' Can you indeed ? ' cried Masborough, with a sparkle of joy in his eyes. ' If you can do that, you will indeed be my saviour. Tell me what you mean.'

' Armenie Sifflet is dead,' said his mother.

The effect of these words upon the duke was magical. He fell back in a chair breathing heavily, and was much agitated.

Mr. Whittaker had taken no part in the conversation. Once or twice he had seemed desirous of speaking, but the duchess waved her hand, so he did not speak.

' Armenie dead,' repeated the duke. ' How do you know that ? '

' Because Jean, her father, has been to me and related the whole affair, begging for more money, as Mr. Hines had overreached himself in stopping the supplies.'

'Then you know all?'

'All. I know how you met this girl Armenie in Baden, and how Hines induced you to marry her in a moment of infatuation and, shall I say, intoxication, and then persuaded you to desert her; I know how he afterwards told you that she was a woman of infamous character, and that it would ruin you to acknowledge her in public, and for that reason you agreed to make her and her father an allowance, on the understanding that they should not molest you. This is the secret of Mr. Hines's power over you, and now that we have proof of Armenie's death we can defy him.'

The duke was profoundly affected.

'My dear mother, I have always known you to be my best friend, and if I have been wanting in affection or duty to you, it is entirely owing to the influence of that man Hines, who has warped me from the proper path. You do not know what I have suffered.'

'Things might have been much worse,' said Mr. Whittaker. 'The fact of the marriage can, I believe, be disputed. You were a Protestant, she a Catholic. However, the great thing is that she is dead and has no power to molest you. Mr. Hines is now like a serpent without a sting.'

'Thank God,' ejaculated the duke, 'this horrible artificial life is over. I am deeply indebted to you, mother, and also to you, Mr. Whittaker, and I fear I have not always treated you with the consideration such a kind friend deserves.'

At this moment Mr. Hines entered the room. He was dressed for the road, having a light dust coat on, and a case containing race glasses slung over his shoulder.

On seeing the duchess and Mr. Whittaker, he bowed with his accustomed politeness, but only met with a cool stare in return.

' Mr. Whittaker, will you oblige me by speaking to this man ? ' said her Grace.

' Certainly, with all the pleasure in the world,' answered Mr. Whittaker.

' Speak to me ? Did I understand your Grace to say that you wished this gentleman to speak to me ? ' exclaimed Mr. Hines.

' Yes, to you.'

' Very well. I am at his service.'

Mr. Hines sat down and disposed himself in a careless attitude to listen to what was coming, not for a moment expecting that a thunderclap was about to burst over his head which would annihilate him.

' In the first place,' said Mr. Whittaker, ' you have acted as the Duke of Masborough's agent. This agency ceases from this hour, and we shall require an account from you. If, as we believe, the accounts are defective, or purposely falsified, they will be examined by competent accountants, and proceedings, if advisable, taken against you in the Criminal Courts.'

' I don't think his Grace will act thus with me,' said Hines, with a sickly smile.

' Have I your authority for speaking as I have done, Masborough ? ' asked Mr. Whittaker.

' Most certainly,' was the duke's reply, in a firm voice.

Going over to his former dupe, Hines hissed in his ear—

' Have you forgotten Baden ? '

' What does he say ? We will have no whispering,' cried Mr. Whittaker.

' He asks me if I have forgotten Baden,' said the duke.

'Do you wish to defy me, all of you?' cried Hines, as he glared round the room.

'We defy you? Yes,' returned the duchess.

'Listen to this. Armenie Sifflet is dead,' Mr. Whittaker exclaimed.

'Dead?' gasped the wretched man.

'We can prove it. Jean has been with us. She is dead. We know that you caused my unfortunate son to marry the poor creature, and you have threatened him ever since that you will put him face to face in London society with his wife, if he thwarted you. Now Armenie is dead, my son can afford to laugh at your threats. Your power is at an end, and you will be compelled by the law to give up your ill-gotten plunder.'

While the duchess was speaking, Mr. Hines grew dangerously pale.

He pressed his hand to his head as if in pain.

His accusers waited for some minutes for him to speak.

Then Mr. Whittaker shook him by the arm, exclaiming—

'Have you nothing to say?'

The man turned a blank expressionless face upon him, and did not appear to recognise him.

'Send for a doctor. He is going to have a fit or some dreadful thing,' the duchess said.

A doctor was sent for, and when he came he heard what had taken place, and having briefly examined Mr. Stoney Hines, exclaimed—

'The shock of this sudden and unexpected revelation acting upon a weak and nervous organisation, has been too much for him.'

'Too much!' repeated Mr. Whittaker.

'Yes; the man is an idiot.'

At this terrible communication, every one turned pale.

The duchess shuddered.

If his faults had been great, his punishment was truly awful.

Mr. Hines now broke into a loud laugh. The doctor spoke to him and he gibed and gibbered in return'; he did not know any one in the room, and his brain seemed to be as much effaced as a slate which has had the figures rubbed off it with a sponge.

He was taken away and placed in a lunatic asylum, where he remained for some years, the Duke of Masborough paying liberally for his support.

We need scarcely say that after this delivery from bad hands, the duke sold his racing establishment, keeping only a few favourite horses. Much of the money that Mr. Hines had robbed him of was returned, and after all no great harm was done. He had his mother to thank for his salvation, and he did not fail to show her that he was grateful for her watchful kindness.

The death of Armenie Sifflet did not grieve the duke because he had never loved her. Mr. Hines, for his own purposes, had induced him to marry her, which he did at an early age, and while half intoxicated.

Mr. Pimplepeck, Mr. Wassett, and Mr. Nicholas Coper were all thrown out of employment by the melancholy collapse of Hines. But they were not long before they found fresh work for idle hands to do in a congenial sphere.

The Duchess of Masborough purposely brought her son in contact again with Miss Emily Arnott.

They had not seen much of one another during the gap of two years, during which his grace had been running his career on the turf, and fancying himself a great man, when as he was in reality a very little one, acting the part of a puppet, the strings of the fantoccini being pulled by Mr. Stoney Hines.

Emily freely forgave him for his want of attention,

and, to the delight of his friends, Masborough married the most charming girl in the country.

So he was saved after all, and one of the grandest old names in the peerage was not dragged through the mire of the bill discounter's office and the bankruptcy court. There was no necessity to write upon an early tombstone, ' He died of sixty per cent.' After his marriage, his Grace devoted himself to politics, and the outside public knowing little or nothing about his affairs, believed that he gave up racing because it interfered with his wish to be a legislator. His speeches in the House of Lords were extensively read and much admired, and Mr. Ommaney Lane Whittaker says, with a smile of satisfaction, ' I always knew that Masborough could not prove untrue to the traditions of his race.'

UNDER THE TERROR;

OR,

A WIFE WITHOUT A HUSBAND.

~~~~~~~~~~~~~~~~~

CHAPTER I.

THE ORDER OF THE DAY.

On the 19th of December, 1793, the Republican army entered Toulon. On the following morning an order of the day, issued by the representatives of the people, strictly enjoined the inhabitants of the city to repair at a certain hour to a large open space, named the Field of Battles. To this order there was no exception. Never before had such an arbitrary and apparently purposeless decree been issued. Men, women, and children, all were to go. In addition to this, everybody was to leave the door of his or her house open, so that patrols, told off for that purpose, could go from street to street and make a house-to-house examination, to satisfy the representatives of the people that none of the population, defying their decree, were concealed in their dwellings.

On the 21st of December, in obedience to the order, the entire population went to the place designated. No wonder that they were disquieted, and that one

F

man scarcely looked another in the face. Rumour as usual was rife, but, although the most alarming reports were in circulation, no one could speak with any certainty as to the object of this collection in mass. The times were troublous, and the general idea was that a wholesale pillage was contemplated. So men whispered to one another. Even influential citizens were afraid to speak loudly, for so many informers, and red-hot Republican agitators, were about, that a few chance words might give a spy sufficient ground whereon to found a charge of treason.

In a word, the people were maddened by this newly found liberty, and the excesses which the Republic allowed them to plunge into all over the country. For this the late government was to blame. France had been shamefully mismanaged, and the people had much to avenge. Unfortunately, to let loose an infuriated public is like raising a floodgate without the means to close it against the torrent of water that you release.

The idea of general pillage found many supporters, because, the city being denuded of its inhabitants, all the shopkeepers being away, and no one left to protect property, the valuable goods would be at the mercy of the soldiery, if they chose to act the part of brigands.

It must be recollected that the Republic had a grudge against Toulon. The conduct of the people had occasioned the country an immense and almost an irreparable loss, for it was alleged against them that they had given to the English its navy and its arsenal, with all the vast stores contained within it. It could be easily understood that the principal citizens would prefer a universal system of plundering to the sanguinary executions to which every part of France was now subjected. Those who entertained this view schooled themselves to find their houses ransacked and rendered desolate on their return, and, in some instances, it was almost laughable to see what miserable countenances those had who tried to be most calm and philosophical under their contemplated misfortune.

Certainly the order was a startling one, but those who had been most guilty in betraying their country by their incapacity and cowardice were most happy in the expectation that their houses would be plundered and their lives spared, for a man can scrape wealth and furniture together, though he be reduced to poverty, if his life be given him. All they were afraid of was being killed. No man's life was safe. The guillotine was rampant, and reared its ghastly head everywhere. No one could make sure to-day of having his head on his shoulders to-morrow. People remembered what had taken place at Lyons. Resistance was futile. Every one walked with an air of resignation. Calamity stared them in the face. This hour they lived, the next they might be dead, or penniless.

As a matter of fact, this was one of the most unheard of and surprising phenomena of this extraordinary epoch. A single man, condemned to death, may not have the spirit to resist the executioner, but a large body of men might be expected to attempt rebellion against an arbitrary decree, which possibly meant extermination. Possibly the fault, which may be called a crime, weighed upon the consciences of the population of Toulon, for they did not endeavour to resist. At the given time every one had come to the vast enclosure of the Field of Battles, and, when all were assembled, the exits were closed and guarded by armed men.

The Toulonaise were prisoners, and several pieces of cannon were turned towards them, the mouths gaping at their midst, threatening to pour in their iron hail at the least movement manifested by the crowd. In addition to this, a double row of soldiers, with fixed

bayonets, encircled them, as if to complete the work
which the artillery might leave unfinished.

A silence resembling that of the grave fell upon all
those mewed up in this huge enclosure. Men could
not speak to their wives, mothers were too terrified to
address their children, or reassure them with kind
words. The women clung to the men for protection,
and strong men wept to think that it was out of their
power to render them any. Many, utterly terrified, exchanged mute adieus by a shaking of the hands. So awful
was the suspense that the crowd thought neither of life
or death. They simply wondered, like those half stunned,
what next would happen. Under the dreadful pressure
put upon them, their faculties were becoming numbed.

Suddenly the roll of the drums broke the silence.

Some assumed a defiant air, some fell on their knees
as if they would make their peace with heaven while
time was yet allowed them. On the faces of all consternation was more than ever depicted.

For a few seconds, it may be safely said, that no
sound interrupted the beat of the drum, except the
scarcely perceptible murmur of ten thousand lips that
prayed. They knew not what might come next. The
cannon might roar and tear them to pieces, the soldiers
might shoot them as they stood, or knock or pierce
them with the bayonet, they knew not, but they prayed.
It was an hour of supreme suspense and peril. The
most hardened supplicated the throne of Grace.

Those who were bold enough to still keep their eyes
open, in a short time perceived a large number of sailors
enter the enclosure; on their hats was written in large
letters, ' Patriots of the Aristides.' The ' Aristides '
was the only vessel which had not given itself up to the
English. The captain in command of the sailors made
extraordinary efforts to avoid dishonour, and it had been
declared in the Assembly that they had deserved well of

the country. The conduct of the ' Aristides ' had been much talked about in Toulon, and when the famous and dreaded name was seen, a panic fear seized possession of those who had hitherto been hopeful. The words ' Patriots of the " Aristides " ' had a terrible significance for the Toulonaise. They meant retribution. Each sailor was accompanied by two soldiers. They walked slowly, looking carefully around them; at intervals they indicated a person by the motion of the hand, and he was instantly dragged out of the enclosure, and shot by a firing squad, in attendance for that purpose. There was no warrant for the arrest, no trial; a butcher could not have picked out with more unconcern certain animals from a herd of bullocks to be led to the slaughter house. The sailors selected people prominent among the townspeople, and all so chosen were immediately shot, as traitors to their country. Some made selections at random : men were pointed out because they were well dressed, and looked like aristocrats, an unpardonable offence just then; others, because of their noble air or defiant bearing, for even in that terrible hour there were those whose bravery supported them; but one man wandered restlessly through the throng, evidently seeking some one particular person. He stood on tip-toe, and looked over the heads of the crowd and there was an expression of anxious ferocity mingled with anticipated revenge upon his rough, unintellectual, battered face; he was like a wild beast searching for prey. The representatives of the people could not have selected a better man to carry out the stern decree, by means of which they had determined to punish the townspeople. At times he would dart forward with outstretched hand, as if he had at last discovered the object of his search, but he would recoil with a disappointed air, as the look of gratified vengeance died out of his gleaming eyes. He had been mistaken. Not yet; he must search further and go wider afield. There were victims enough at hand, had he desired indiscriminate bloodshed; but he was evidently searching for an enemy, and the rage burning in his face showed that he would not relax his energy until he was found.

The day crept on; the firing was not so frequent as it had been at first, the 'Patriots of the "Aristides"' were becoming glutted, and people stared wonderingly, or drew back in awe when this sailor passed them, gazing at them with fiendish curiosity: the task of blood was nearly accomplished. The representatives of the people were considering the propriety of announcing by a fresh roll of the drums that justice was appeased, when one sailor stopped suddenly before a young girl, and pointing her out to a soldier, said, 'That is she.'

At those words the girl looked up, as if wondering to whom they applied; they were of dire import, and she knew well enough sounded the knell of some one. This indifference increased the anger of the sailor, who cried more loudly than before, 'Take her away; have I not said that she is the one?' Then she regarded the sailor with a fixed stare, in which there was no recognition. She was astonished, that was all, and her accuser was rendered furious at her apparent indifference. Evidently wishing her to know who he was, he addressed her in an insolent tone —

'I am Jean Poyer,' he said; 'you know me now. Come, prepare; you are to die.' He eagerly awaited the effect of his words.

'Jean Poyer,' she replied in a puzzled voice, and she said the name over to herself, as if trying to recall it; but eventually she bowed her head, to indicate that her memory would not serve her.

'Away with her,' cried the sailor with a tigerish look, leaning toward her as if he could himself have been her executioner.

' Mind what you are about, perhaps you may be mistaken,' said the soldier who accompanied him.

Jean Poyer retired a few steps to carefully survey the soldier who was audacious enough to call his will in question, and said, ' I tell you, it is she !'

' Who ?' asked the soldier, grounding his musket, as if anxious to provoke a colloquy which might save the girl.

' Who ? Why Miss Carmélite de Brissac. Do you think I don't know her ?'

' That is my name,' said the young lady, mildly.

' You see,' said the sailor, ' she does not deny it ; take her away, and let her be shot like the rest.'

The soldier knew that it was dangerous to resist the order of any sailor of the ' Aristides,' but a very strange sympathy had sprung up in his rugged heart, which beat warmly beneath his uniform, for the defenceless creature. He would have taken a man to death without a scruple. He had killed the enemies of his country on the battle field, but a woman, a mere girl—'twas a different affair altogether.

' What has she done to deserve to be shot ?' he asked.

' Never mind; that is my business. I order it. I Jean Poyer, able seaman, and patriot of the "Aristides."'

The crowd grew denser round the disputants and their victim ; murmurs of approbation arose at the soldier's boldness, when another ' Aristides' man came up, and carelessly inquired of his messmate what was the matter.

' Matter enough,' replied Jean Poyer. ' This military traitor refuses to obey my commands and conduct an aristocrat to execution.'

' Ah !' observed the second sailor, regarding Miss de Brissac with an air of admiration ; ' she is pretty, and the soldier has good taste.'

As he spoke, he took the liberty of raising her chin, and looking more closely at her delicate skin and regular features. Great as was his rudeness, she did not dare to protest, it was an age of license, and she was powerless; besides, the fear of death encompassed her, and she was like one stunned by a sudden calamity.

'I'll save her if she likes to put herself in my wake and hoist Republican colours,' continued he.

'Neither you nor any one else shall save her,' cried Jean Payer, furiously; 'her life is forfeited, because I, exercising my right, have ordered her to be shot!'

'I don't know about that,' said the sailor, measuring his antagonist with his eye.

'Then I shall have to make you,' replied Payer, whose wrath was for the moment diverted from one object to another.

It was evident these men, though serving in the same ship, were not on friendly terms. Their faces expressed mutual hate and distrust; the one who had interfered felt an unmistakable pleasure in trying to thwart his shipmate, and the crowd, anticipating a contest between them, gladly drew back on all sides, hoping that a favourable diversion for the young lady had been created by the mere accident.

It may be interesting to describe Jean Payer, who was a man of about forty years of age, rather short and thickset; his limbs were big, his chest broad, and the muscles standing out on his arms denoted great physical strength; his face was flat and scarred, his forehead low and almost brutal, his hair red, and his expression was one of stupid ferocity, helped out with a dash of low cunning. He had the brute force common to such low mental developments, and looked contemptuously at his adversary, who was ten years his junior, tall, thin, and not unpleasing in appearance; his hair was black as a raven's plumage, and though he had no superfluous flesh about him, it was pretty evident that he was

muscular, and knew his own power. Poyer seemed to
have enfeebled himself by the excessive use of spirits,
for his cheeks were red and his blood heated. The other
from his pallor looked more temperate. Both wore
coloured kerchiefs round their necks, tied in a knot,
and both had large gold earrings pendant from
their ears. One was a type of the sailor of Lower
Brittany, low, coarse, brutal; the other a Provencal,
not yet wholly corrupted. One was middle-aged, the
other young; one plain, the other good-looking, if not
handsome. The courage of one was cool and confident,
that of the other, boastful and rash. They were born on
the banks of rival rivers, among populations which
habitually disputed with one another for maritime
supremacy, that is to say, for the palm which the country accorded to the best sailors. They had every reason
in the world to hate one another, and they did hate
most cordially.

Jean Poyer took off his jacket and handed it to a
by-stander; his kerchief he rolled up and placed in
his pocket, then he tightened his belt, while his antagonist made similar preparations.

'You are determined to save this aristocrat, Nicholas?' he said.

'As for that, I care little enough about her,' replied
the sailor. 'You and I have an old score to settle,
and——'

'You shall not be disappointed, I say it on the word
of a man,' interrupted Jean eagerly. 'Just give me
five minutes while I see this traitress to the Republic
shot, and I am with you. Wait here, or appoint
any place of meeting you like; there's my hand on
it.'

It is highly probable that Nicholas would have com-
plied with this request had he not caught Miss Carmelite de Brissac's expressive eyes fixed upon him with

such a supplicating expression that he could not resist their mute prayer.

'No,' he returned doggedly, clenching his fists, ' now or never.'

The Bas-Breton set his teeth together, and, without further parley, landed himself upon Nicholas with a violence that threatened to exterminate him, but a soldier—the one, indeed, who had first befriended Miss de Brissac in the first instance—drew him on one side, and Jean was carried by the impetus of his attack into the middle of the crowd, who hooted and jeered at him. Quickly recovering himself, he was again before Nicholas, and a terrible struggle began between those two men.

Then it was that the soldier made his way to the young lady's side, and said in a whisper—

'Escape! Now is your time!'

She did not remain to be advised twice, and, finding that the soldier was really in earnest in his determination to save her, she glided away through the densely packed crowd; at the same moment the drums sounded the recall of the patriots of the " Aristides." The carnival of slaughter was over.

At this sound, which, infuriated as they were, they had the sense to recognize and obey, the two sailors separated, disfigured and hurt. Jean Poyer looked around him, and, failing to see his victim, a cry like that of a wild beast in the extremity of hunger escaped him. Turning to the soldier he said—

'At least I know you. It is through you this has happened, and you shall pay for her, I swear it!'

'Never fear,' exclaimed Nicholas. 'We are friends now, you and I. He has knocked me about like an old hogshead, and I will not help him to identify and establish a charge against you. Never fear, I say, he shall not hurt you, though the coward would have you made shorter by a head.'

' Very well,' ejaculated Poyer, who directed himself towards that part of the enclosure where the representtatives of the people were assembled, ' we shall see.'

Nicholas followed him more slowly, uttering continued menaces, for he had come worst off in the encounter. At the same time the soldier fell back sadly, and took his place in the ranks, with the unpleasant consciousness that, by interfering to save the life of an aristocrat and a suspect, he had placed his own in jeopardy. It would have been better for him had he obeyed the orders of the fierce patriot of the good ship " Aristides."

CHAPTER II.

SERGEANT BERBINS.

In the evening of that sad December day, which had put half Toulon into mourning, the representatives of the people, Albitte, Salicetti and Barras, were closeted together, to consider what ulterior measures should be taken for the re-organisation of the city, when they were informed that the patriots of the 'Aristides' demanded to see them. As those men had played such an important part in what may be called the ceremony of the day, it was decided to admit them at once. Jean Poyer was first introduced to the three members of the Convention, and he told his tale. A soldier had refused to seize an aristocrat in obedience to his orders, and she had escaped. Nicholas appeared in his turn, having come to defend the soldier as he had promised, and having heard his story, the representatives of the people were slightly embarrassed how to decide between two such distinguished patriots. At length Barras hit upon a middle course, and addressing himself first to Jean, said, ' Citizen patriot, your zeal shall be recompensed, you shall achieve the death of the woman you have proscribed ; find her out, and she shall be executed on the spot.'

Then turning to Nicholas he continued—

' As to you, my brave citizen, you shall also be recompensed. The soldier who has dared to disobey Jean Poyer deserves to be punished with death. We place his life in your hands. If you denounce him he shall be led to the guillotine.'

After this decision the patriots were shown to the door Jean discontented enough, because he had no means of tracing Miss de Brissac. Nicholas feeling that he had so far triumphed, since the soldier's life was at his disposal. As they came out of the Prefecture, Jean said—

' I will have her head in spite of you.'

And Nicholas replied—

' I will save the soldier's in spite of you.'

And they separated mutually defiant.

Two days after this scene, a review of the troops in garrison was held on the Field of Battles. The soldier who had incurred Jean Poyer's displeasure was in the ranks, he had not been out of barracks for two days, fearing that some denunciation might overtake him, for the sailor had shown himself to be a vindictive person with a good memory. In fact, Jean had been searching for the soldier; he came to the conclusion that he might know something about Miss de Brissac, and be induced to give up her address; as he had vainly searched through the city without finding any trace of her, he was baffled. Hearing of the review, Jean went to the Field of Battles and walked up and down to discover the soldier without success, but the latter saw him, and guessed for whom he was looking; he became very much frightened, thinking that he intended to denounce him, not knowing that his life was safe in Nicholas's hands so long as the two shipmates continued enemies. In a short time the representatives of the people appeared on the scene with the staff, and those men who had distinguished themselves in late actions with the enemy were called forward and rewarded. At length they came to the battalion to which the soldier belonged. He heard a name called, Pierre Berbins. It was his own. His knees shook, and all the blood deserted his cheeks.   He, who had never felt a particle of fear in battle, exhibited all the signs of extreme cowardice, for he thought he was to be punished for his chivalrous behaviour towards a proscribed aristocrat.   Seeing that he did not move, his sergeant-major exclaimed—

'Here, Pierre Berbins, do you not hear yourself called ?   Step forward, by your right, march.   In obedience to the word of command, the soldier quitted the rear rank in which he was placed, and advanced slowly, not at all reassured to see Jean Poyer amongst the spectators ; arrived before Barras, he bent his head imagining that sentence of death was about to be passed upon him.   But to his astonishment the representative said, Pierre Berbins, the French Republic, one and indi-visible, wishes to recompence those who have served it it with courage and fidelity ; for your patriotism and bravery, I name you sergeant of the company to which you belong.

Pierre saluted in military fashion, and extending his arm received the stripes which indicated his rank. Then he rejoined his companions, not without casting a furtive glance to the corner in which he had re-marked the Bas-Breton sailor.

It appeared that Pierre Berbins had well deserved the promotion which had been accorded him, for he was received with cheers from all in the battalion ; but the poor fellow was ill at ease, twenty cannons would not have made him quail, yet the mere thought of the guillotine unmanned him.   He did not feel himself safe, he fancied that a great danger menaced him, and an icy sweat broke out on his brow, when Jean Poyer waved his hand in token of recognition.

Soon the attention of his comrades and of the crowd was attracted by fresh promotions ; nothing, however, could remove the preoccupation of Sergeant Berbins, whose want of enthusiasm struck every one as peculiar, and his dread increased when the company marched back to barracks, for he saw Jean Poyer place himself near the band, as if to follow it home and not lose sight of Berbins. Jean was at the gate as the men marched in, and his rough voice exclaimed, ' Good-day, my sergeant! when you have done inside, then come out here, I have two words to say to you.'

When the men were dismissed, the majority went to put away their arms, but Pierre remained sad and silent in the middle of the courtyard, resting upon his musket. The captain, with whom he was a great favourite, approached him, and slapping him on the shoulder, said, ' What are you thinking of, eh ?' The equality and fraternity prevalent in those days among the Republicans rendered such a proceeding perfectly natural.

The sergeant started, and recognising his superior officer, pointed to the barrack gates which stood open, and permitted the figure of Jean Poyer to be discerned almost on the threshold.

' Look at that fellow,' he exclaimed, in a voice in which fear struggled with rage. ' I should like to run him through with my bayonet ; better do that and stop his further power for mischief, even if I am shot. The prospect of being shot is preferable to that of being guillotined for saving the girl's life.'

' What nonsense are you talking ?' inquired the captain. ' You must be cautious how you attack patriots like the sailors of the "Aristides." They have much power, and can be dangerous if they like.'

' Ah ! you don't know all, but I will tell you, viscount, when I have an opportunity.'

' Call me captain,' hastily said the officer; ' you know there are no titles now—forget that I was the Viscount D'Evreux. It would an offence in that sailor's hearing to address me by my title. I cannot imagine what has happened to you within the last two days. Have you lost your head? You have not been the same man.'

'I have not yet become quite stupid, but I cannot answer for myself if this goes on much longer.'

'To what do you allude?' asked Captain D'Evreux.

'That rascal's persecution,' replied Pierre.

'Why does he persecute you?'

'For saving the young lady's life on the Field of Battles two days ago. I will tell you all about it in a few words, then you shall judge whether or not the mere sight of that man is not enough to make me feel ill.'

Pierre Berbins proceeded to recount the whole adventure. In the first place he had been told off to accompany Jean Poyer. Secondly, they encountered a young lady who was demanded by Jean. Thirdly, Nicholas arrived opportunely, and created a diversion in her favour which enabled her to escape, though Pierre was no doubt answerable to the public for disobedience of orders in the beginning of the affair.

Captain D'Evreux became more and more thoughtful as the sergeant proceeded with his narrative, and Pierre fancied it was owing to his sympathy for him, and went on, 'You see in what a miserable position I am placed, my life is not worth a day's purchase;' a tear trembled in his eye, and as he dashed it away with the back of his hand, a rough voice exclaimed, 'I say, citizen sergeant, how much longer are you going to keep me waiting out here. I shall take root and begin to grow soon!'

'You hear him, captain?' said the sergeant.

'Yes, he wishes to speak to you; hear what he has to say.'

'But he wishes to denounce me, to drag me to the

guillotine for stepping between him and the life of this unlucky aristocrat!'

'Well,' said Captain D'Evreux, 'if that is his intention, your refusal to see him will make no difference.'

Jean Poyer did not wait any longer for permission to enter the barrack yard; he walked straight in, like a man who has business with some one, and going up to the officer, said, in an undertone, ' Is it against orders, citizen captain, for a soldier to answer when he is spoken to ?'

At this mode of address D'Evreux's face expressed disgust and indignation, but controlling himself, he replied, ' You have served in the navy, citizen sailor, and you know that military duties must be attended to.'

' That's very likely; yet he might have cried out, " Coming presently."'

' Very well; presently,' said D'Evreux, motioning him off with impatience.

Jean Poyer was not to be disposed of so easily; he shrugged his shoulders and clenched his fist, which was a sign that he was getting angry.

' Do you hear me ?' asked Captain D'Evreux.

' I hear you fast enough,' answered Jean.

' In that case be off.'

' Who is to make me go ?' said Jean defiantly.

' Who ?' repeated the captain, laying his hand on the hilt of his sword.

' Yes,' boldly continued Jean; ' who dare lay a finger upon a patriot of the " Aristides ?"'

The captain took a step towards the insolent fellow, but the sergeant, apprehending serious consequences, threw himself between them, crying—

' Take care what you do, viscount.'

' Ha! ha!' laughed Jean on hearing this, ' have we found a nest of aristocrats? The guillotine is a good

eater ; one cannot feed her too much, and her favourite
food is the peerage.'

'Away with you,' exclaimed Sergeant Berbins, losing
his temper. 'Quick march ! go, or I shall have to help
you with the point of my bayonet. Now then, half
turn to the right—by your left, march !'

'Oh, it is like that, is it ?' answered Jean unmoved.
'You seem to be very courageous since Nicholas begged
your life from the representative Barras.'

'What ?' gasped Berbins, scarcely able to credit the
good news.

'It cuts both ways,' continued Jean Poyer. 'Nicholas got your life, and I got Miss Carmélite de Brissac's.
She shall not escape me the next time I come across
her.'

'Miss de Brissac,' cried Captain D'Evreux, with an
air of the most lively interest. 'Is all this fuss about
Miss de Brissac ?'

'Do you know her, captain ?' exclaimed Jean, forgetting his habitual Republican insolence. 'If you will
only tell me where to find her, or, if you don't like to
betray a friend, just give me a clue to her address, I'll
follow the track like a sleuth hound, and I will be your
devoted servant for life. Excuse the way in which I
speak, I am excited. Tell me where I can find this
woman, and I will go all over the town with your name
on my lips, and proclaim you the greatest patriot in the
whole army.'

Captain D'Evreux had an opportunity of recovering
from his first surprise while Jean was talking with
volubility, and he said to him, with an air of friendly
familiarity—

'Do you want to speak to Berbins to find out that ?'

'Yes, captain. He ought to know where she is,
because he saved her,' Jean Poyer answered.

'But I did not actually save her,' hastily said the

sergeant. ' I only remonstrated with you against taking
the life of a woman, who certainly did not recognise
you. It was Nicholas who stepped in between you.
As a matter of fact I do not know where she lives.'

' Truly ? '

' Truly ! I swear it, by my love for our common
country.'

' Then I must search elsewhere,' said Jean, with a
crestfallen and dejected air. ' I made sure she was
some friend of yours, or you would never have interfered.'

' Stop a moment,' exclaimed the Viscount D'Evreux.
' Let us put our heads together, perhaps our united
efforts may be successful. I, too, want to discover the
beautiful Carmélite de Brissac.'

' You know her Christian name, do you?' Jean Poyer
remarked with a suspicious air.

' Thou seest ! ' replied the captain, affecting the fami-
liar *tutoiment*, or ' thoning,' then in vogue. ' Thou
seest, citizen, that I know the lady.'

' And you want to find her ? '

' Certainly.'

' To save her perhaps ? '

' Thou insultest me, citizen. When it is a question of
" shortening " an aristocrat, you will always find me a
good patriot.'

Pierre opened his eyes to their fullest extent, but
receiving a look from his captain, he cried, ' The
captain is right ; may I be shot if I know what in-
fluenced me in interesting myself on behalf of this
aristocrat. I go for the Republic, one and indivisible,
or death. It is my duty. I have taken an oath to that
effect, and I mean to keep it.'

The Viscount D'Evreux shrugged his shoulders, and
exclaimed, ' Citizen sailor, we seem to be agreed in this
matter : will you do me the pleasure to ascend to my

chamber with the sergeant? You can tell us why you hunt down Miss de Brissac, and we will combine our efforts to find her.'

'That's right enough,' said Jean.

'And as nothing makes one's throat so dry as talking, do you, sergeant, send up to my room half-a-dozen bottles of wine.'

'And a bottle of brandy,' put in the sailor.

'Do you like brandy?' asked the captain.

'Yes, after drinking wine, a glass or two of brandy makes one sober.'

The sailor and the captain ascended the stairs of the officer's quarters together; Pierre soon rejoined them with the wine and brandy. The fire was made up, and they all three drew their chairs near the table, on which stood the uncorked bottles.

CHAPTER III.

THE SAILOR'S STORY.

'As you know Miss de Brissac,' began the sailor, 'I need not tell you that her family lived in Brest, which is also my native town. I began my naval career under the ex-king. The Baron de Brissac commanded my ship. I love the sea, and was a good sailor, but I did not like the aristocrat De Brissac. The regulations of the service were very strict, and, knowing the consequences of mutinous conduct, I put up with many slights, indignities, and injustice, though much against my will. Soon after our captain's daughter was born, he became furiously jealous of his wife. She bore him a son, and he effected a separation. His temper became worse than ever, and we had to suffer for his domestic unhappiness. Never did a crew put up with a greater martinet. When his daughter was four years old he took her on board with her nurse. We set sail with them. This was contrary to orders, but the authorities took no notice of it. Every one knew that the baron thought that his wife had been unfaithful to him, and, in fact, an aristocrat could do what he liked in those days. Live the Republic!'

Jean emptied his glass, filled it, and emptied it again.

'Ah,' said M. D'Evreux, 'I begin to see the cause of your hatred to Miss de Brissac.'

'My hatred for Miss de Brissac?' repeated Jean; 'I don't hate her, it is her father I would exterminate.'

'But, not being able to revenge yourself upon him, you determine to condemn the daughter to death?' inquired D'Evreux.

'Exactly. The old rascal is in England, but he will learn that his old sailor, Jean Poyer, has caused his favourite child to be executed. He loves her so much that this will be a severe blow to him. He would rather die himself than any harm should befall her.'

D'Evreux elevated his eyebrows as if in surprise, and the Bas-Breton continued—

'I assure you, for this voyage, the captain was like a wild beast. If one committed the least fault it was followed by the most terrible punishments. He did not seem to sleep, he was always on deck, running about here, and poking his nose there, like a poisoned rat. We resembled cattle. He took no more heed of us than if we had been beasts of the field. But one day a change took place, and this is how it happened. I was leaning against a gun, kicking my heels, and thinking that Miss Carmélite's nurse was uncommonly pretty. She was from Brittany, you know, and they are fine women all about there. Suddenly I felt a blow on the back, which sent me staggering some distance. I turned round with a bound, my fists clenched like bolts of iron. It was the captain.

' " What have you to say ? " he asked, regarding me curiously.

'I was half out of my mind, and, thinking of nothing so much as what the whole ship's company had to put up with, replied—

' " If your wife has made a fool of you, it is no reason why you should revenge yourself upon a sailor." '

'You said that?' cried Viscount D'Evreux, as if all his gentleman's pride and vanity was interested in the injury given to another gentleman, for at this moment it was not the Republican captain who hob-nobbed with the citizen sailor, so much as it was the nobleman who tolerated the boor. 'You said that, and he did not either throw you overboard, or run his sword through your body!'

Perhaps this remark recalled Jean to the old rule, for he answered, 'Directly I had spoken, I expected either one or the other. He became pale, looking at me with eyes that glowed like red-hot coals. I began to be afraid! but it passed away.

' "You are right, Jean," he said, "you were not in fault."

' Then he went below and did not come on deck any more the whole day; after this he became a different man, or rather the man he was before, cold and severe, capricious perhaps, but not an intolerable tyrant. He never found fault with me, and the first lieutenant was equally kind; my shipmates congratulated me on my pluck and my good fortune, and one night I heard our chaplain say to the first lieutenant—our chaplain was the Abbé d'Arvilliers——'

' D'Arvilliers!' cried the viscount, interrupting the recital again. 'John, the present bishop of that name?'

' The same, he was a relation of Miss de Brissac's.'

' And consequently of Carmélite, I mean of the captain's daughter?'

' Precisely; do you know him also?' asked Jean, bending his gaze critically on the captain.

' Only by name; he was condemned to death by the revolutionary tribunal at Nantes, and I believe escaped with other " emigrants " to Coblentz.'

' That's him,' answered Jean.

' Well, what did he say to the first officer?'

' " It seems to me," he observed, "that the remark of this sailor has had as great an effect upon the captain as if a voice had spoken to him out of a cloud. It was more powerful than all my exhortations; just a few words of truth spoken at random have recalled him to himself." '

'You will see that I had not done any harm by speaking as I did. Every one applauded me. We were all better treated. Everything went as if on wheels. I suspected nothing, but that fellow Nicholas, who was one of my shipmates, always kept on saying, "Look out for squalls, Jean." '

'The same who fought with you the other day?' asked Pierre Berbins.

'That is the identical one; he was then Captain de Brissac's cabin boy and high in his master's favour.'

'Did he recognise Miss de Brissac that day on the Field of Battles?' inquired D'Evreux.

'No. I was particularly careful not to mention her name before him. He left the frigate when he was fourteen, and she was then a child of four and a-half, or thereabouts, so that he had very little chance of knowing her again.'

Captain D'Evreux remarked with pleasure that the sailor applied himself quite as diligently to the task of emptying the bottles, as he did to the recital of his story.

'I tell you,' continued Jean, 'that I was as happy as a fish in the sea, doing almost as I liked, and making love to Mariole, the nurse of Miss de Brissac. She gave me every encouragement, and I dreamt of marrying her if she would have me. I fancied that she was madly in love with me, as I certainly was with her, and we made each other little presents. I gave her a cross of gold which had belonged to my mother, and she presented me with half a dozen handkerchiefs of real silk. Well, one morning there was a terrible row in the ship; a robbery, they said, had been committed. The staff assembled, and an inquiry was made. They went all over the ship; they searched the chests and the bunks of the seamen. I was struck dumb with surprise when I heard what they said after going to mine.'

' " The thief is discovered. It is Jean Poyer."

' " Who called me a thief ? " I cried.

' " I," answered the officer in the command ; " Mariole has declared that half a dozen silk handkerchiefs have been stolen from the captain's cabin, and here they are in your chest."

' You might have knocked me down with a feather. I saw it all now, but putting a bold face on the matter I struggled to believe in Mariole's honesty.

' " It is not true. She could not say that ! " I exclaimed.

' " We shall see ; put him in irons," answered the officer.

' For three days I was kept upon bread and water, and I had ample time to reflect upon my position. It seemed incredible that Mariole, my Mariole, whom I had fondly hoped to make my wife, and with whom I was madly in love, could have betrayed me ; yet, what other conclusion could I come to. The time came when I was brought before the court-martial. Nicholas laughed at me as I descended the hatchway leading to the captain's cabin. Then I began to suspect that Captain de Brissac had laid a trap for me, and the boy knew it all along. I at once told the court that I believed I was the victim of the captain's vengeance. I said that I had alluded to his wife's infidelity, and therefore he hated me in secret. The president bade me be silent. Mariole gave her evidence weeping, but she said that she did not give me the silk handkerchiefs. My messmates had seen me leave my hammock in the night to speak to Mariole ; as for Nicholas, the little scamp said he knew nothing at all. The end of it was that I was condemned to run the gauntlet and to ten

years at the galleys. Any other man would have died
under the first punishment, for they did not spare me;
the rascals hit with all their might. I ran the broad-
side of the whole crew six times, but I had that within
which sustained me. It was the hope of vengeance; I
swore that I would live to be revenged upon Captain
De Brissac. I was certain that he had induced Mariole to
accuse me. Far from forgetting or forgiving the insult
that I had given him, he treasured it up in his heart,
and obtained a punishment for me infinitely more
severe than any he, in his capacity, could inflict.
When they sent me from the ship I was a living sore,
from the hurts they had given me while running the
gauntlet; nevertheless I served my ten years. You
have never been in a convict prison and cannot imagine
the misery I have undergone. Instead of killing one
aristocrat it is a wonder I did not insist upon slaughter-
ing a hundred. What made my punishment the
more irksome was the knowledge that I did not deserve
it. A man who plans and perpetrates a robbery calcu-
lates the possible profit and the ultimate risk. If he
fails he has not much to grumble at; with me it was
different. Captain De Brissac, directly after the court-
martial, transferred Nicholas to another ship and sent
his child on shore, giving her into the care of his relative
Miss D'Arvilliers, the sister of our chaplain, who lives
at Orient, where she was brought up and educated. I
am informed that she had been sent here to rejoin her
father, who was in the roadstead of Toulon, and who
was one of the wretches who gave up the fleet to the
English, and he fled when your troops entered the town.'

'Did he go alone?' asked Captain D'Evreux.

'I cannot tell. Some say that the bishop has gone
to Coblentz with the other emigrants, as I told you
just now, and others declare that De Brissac and
D'Arvilliers are together.'

'Then why did not Miss De Brissac go with her father?'

'That,' answered Jean Poyer, 'is what I cannot tell you. All I know for certain is, they were seen together in Toulon, and the day we took possession of the town they escaped. A friend of mine assisted them, and informed me that he was to be paid for doing so. He heard their conversation, and told me, because he knew that I owed all my misfortunes to a De Brissac. They had a firm hope that the daughter was safe, and would come overland to a port near England and join them in that country. This course they imagined to be safer than taking her with him in a frail bark, more especially as she had influential friends in Toulon. So you see that though the father has escaped me, I can still put my hand on the daughter.'

'That seems fair enough,' answered D'Evreux, 'but how are you to catch her? You know Toulon well, I suppose—have you any idea of a place where she is likely to hide?'

'If I had any idea I shouldn't want your assistance,' replied Jean, helping himself again and again, and beginning to stutter in his speech.

'Of course, yet if you will tell us the quarters you have searched, we will try other directions.'

'I have been everywhere.'

'Everywhere? even in the lowest streets of the town?'

'What's the use of looking in low streets for Miss De Brissac?' replied Jean with a drunken laugh; 'she wouldn't go into the lowest part of the town, not she.'

'You are right again,' said D'Evreux, with a peculiar smile; 'wait till to-morrow, and I will promise you on the word of a Republican to do all I can to find her.'

'That's settled,' answered Jean Poyer, finishing the

bottle of brandy. 'Let it rest there. You are good patriots. Hurrah for the Republic !—one, and indivisible—that or death ! '

His head soon fell upon his hands, which were already placed upon the table, and, after muttering a few incoherent words, he began to snore with a certain amount of regularity and profundity.

CHAPTER IV.

CAPTAIN D'EVREUX'S SECRET.

WHEN Captain D'Evreux was satisfied that the sailor had cast anchor, he made a sign to his sergeant, and they quitted the room together.

'What next?' said Berbins, addressing the captain when they were outside.

'We must save this young lady,' answered D'Evreux.

'I could see that was your idea from the first, but in order to do so, we must know where she is.'

'I can tell you. She is in the sailors' quarter, in one of the worst streets of the town, where no one would think of looking for her. The sailor is mistaken in supposing that the bishop has escaped to Coblentz. Baron De Brissac and he are together, and will shortly, I trust, reach England in safety. I have been in constant communication with Miss De Brissac, and did not imagine that she was in any immediate danger. The discovery I have just made is fortunate, for I will take instant steps to protect her.'

'The sailor is terribly incensed against her father, and will not spare her on any account,' remarked the sergeant.

'I can see that he has brooded over his revenge.'

'He was unjustly accused and has been wronged. Ten years at the galleys for an imaginary crime would sour any man's temper.'

'Yes,' said D'Evreux, thoughtfully. 'The aristocracy abused their power shamefully, and they are now reaping the harvest they sowed.'

'You can command me,' continued Pierre, 'only tell me what you wish me to do.'

'Keep this Jean Poyer in my room until I return. I am going to see Miss De Brissac, and assure myself that she is safe and comfortable,' replied the young captain.

He took a few steps towards the staircase and suddenly stopped.

'I have changed my mind,' he continued; 'you shall go to Miss De Brissac for me. I will guard this drunken fellow.'

He hastily scribbled the address of the house in which Miss Carmelite was staying on a scrap of paper, which he handed to Pierre.

'Are you afraid I should chatter?' asked the latter, with a reproachful glance.

'No. I am satisfied that my secret is safe with you, but it is better for a sergeant to enter such a house, than an officer in uniform. My presence there in daylight might excite suspicion; at all events it would give rise to remark, and there are spies about.'

'Who am I to ask for?'

'Louise Feron, at the address I have given you. Assure Miss De Brissac that all goes well; her friends are watching over her. As soon as possible, efforts will be made to get her into Germany.'

'I will go,' said the sergeant, 'though we are playing with edged tools. I hope no evil will come of it for either of us, captain.'

The soldier departed, and the captain remained motionless on the landing for some little time wrapped in thought. Then he re-entered his room, and found the sailor snoring in a manner anything but melodious. Presently he began to arrange some clothes and other articles in a portmanteau, as if preparing for instant flight, should it be necessary. In a drawer was a purse full of gold; he distributed the pieces in various pockets. While he was thus engaged Pierre re-entered, and at once saw his design.

'Pardon me, viscount,' he said, in a rough manner, 'I can see what is in your mind. You intend to fly with Miss De Brissac, and as for me, if all is discovered, I may be left for the guillotine.'

'What has put that idea in your head?' asked Viscount D'Evreux, uneasily.

'Circumstances have forced you to accept a commission in the Republican army, but your heart is not with us. You are noble, and your sympathies are with the aristocrats and the emigrants. I am a peasant and a true patriot. It is different with you. I will, however, place no obstacle in your way. You are right to be watchful, if you would save the unhappy lady in whom we both take an interest. She is in danger at this moment, for the other sailor has found her out.

'Which other?' asked D'Evreux, in great consternation.

'Nicholas.'

At the mention of this name, Jean Poyer started and moved uneasily. It must have had a strange attraction for him, as Pierre spoke in a low voice.

'Where is Nicholas?' he cried, sitting up.

Looking around him, he only saw the captain and the sergeant, and leant back in his chair.

'Who spoke of Nicholas? What has he done now?' he continued.

'He is boasting that he will save the aristocrat,' answered the sergeant.

'Oh! he says so, does he?' replied Jean. 'I must find the rascal out and exterminate him; he should not boast.'

He rose and endeavoured to walk to the door, staggering against the wall as he did so.

'That will not be difficult,' Pierre went on, for I left him at the first cabarat on the quay; he was saying that he had beaten you in fair fight, and added that you should not kick a dog without his permission.

These words excited Jean to the pitch of desperation; he rushed to the door, and Pierre, making a sign to the captain, assisted him down stairs, across the barrack yard, and through the gate, and had the satisfaction of seeing him go away with an unsteady gait, vowing vengeance against his enemy Nicholas.

When the sergeant returned, D'Evreux said, 'Why did you enrage him against Nicholas?'

'In the first place, I thought it advisable to get rid of him. I have not seen Nicholas, so if they meet it will be by accident: as for that, if they killed one another, it would be no great misfortune. Secondly,—'

'Tell me about Miss De Brissac,' interrupted the captain, impatiently.

'She recognised and thanked me warmly for what I had done for her on the Field of Battles,' answered the sergeant, 'and made many kind enquiries after you. It is evident with whom she is in love.'

'How was she discovered?' enquired D'Evreux, turning away his face, which grew flushed.

'Nicholas was strolling along the street and saw her at a window to which she had imprudently ventured. He immediately cried out, 'There is the aristocrat, Jean Poyer would give something to see her. It would be look out for the Magdalene. He seemed to make a note of the address, and as she shrank back from the window she saw him go on his way chuckling to himself as if he had made a great discovery, which pleased him mightily.'

'How long is this ago!'

' About a couple of hours. Miss de Brissac is in a terrible fright, and begged me to ask you to visit her as soon as possible, for she thinks her life is not safe.'

' We must find another lodging for her at once,' said D'Evreux, shortly.

' I should not think she would be at all sorry to get out of the horrible neighbourhood in which she is. The landlady lets her have her room to herself, and she is not disturbed; yet the language she must hear in the street is dreadful for a young lady born and educated as she has been.'

' You are right there,' answered the captain, grating his teeth together harshly.

' Your pardon, viscount,' said Pierre, after a pause; ' we have no time to lose ! '

' Thank you for recalling me to myself,' replied D'Evreux. ' The misery this unfortunate girl has had to put up with distracts me. I need not tell you that I love her, and I have every reason to believe that she is as fondly attached to me as I am to her.'

' I believe that,' cried Pierre Berbins.

' I have known her and her family for some years now. Indeed, we were acquainted in happier times, when we laughed at Lafayette and Mirabeau, and never dreampt of the murder of the king, nor the capture of the Bastille. A more amiable, good, virtuous and accomplished girl never breathed.'

' It is sad to think that her life should be endangered, because her father abused his power, and acted tyrannically. We must not underrate the danger she runs, and I will tell you in what way. At present Jean Poyer and Nicholas are at enmity, but drunken, dissolute fellows, such as they are, may make up their difference in the first cabaret in which they meet; suppose they shake hands, suppose they exchange confidences, and Nicholas tells the other where to find Miss de Brissac. The

H

peril is pressing. Come with me and let us do the best
we can without any further delay.

They quitted the barracks at once and walked quickly
along. The captain stopped before a house where
apartments were to be let. It was nicely situated, and
in a respectable street.

' Go in and take lodgings for Miss de Brissac in her
own name,' exclaimed D'Evreux, giving the sergeant
some money. ' Pay in advance and select rooms at the
back of the house, for a woman left by herself all day
grows tired and will look into the street. Wait here
till I come back, I will go and fetch Carmelite.'

Sergeant Berbins did as he was told. The people of
the house willingly let the room, and received payment
in advance. The sergeant bought a few necessary
articles of grocery, and in half an hour D'Evreux
returned, leading Miss de Brissac thickly veiled and
leaning heavily on his arm, as if for protection and
support. Berbins waited outside the door until
D'Evreux sought him.

' All is well so far,' said the captain. ' I have to
thank you for your zeal. Go back to barracks, and if
I am inquired for say I shall probably not be in to-
night.'

' Then you intend—that is you hope—? '

' This very night,' said the captain. ' I cannot leave
her by herself. If I can get a boat and a couple of
men about midnight.'

' I see,' exclaimed Berbins, ' you need not say anything more, captain. I wish you success. Think
sometimes of the sergeant who risked so much for
you. May you both be happy.'

Viscount D'Evreux wrung the honest fellow's hand
and he took his departure for the barracks.

The night was stormy, and rain fell at intervals. At
ten o'clock the next morning, the captain had not made

his appearance, and Serjeant Berbins came to the conclusion that he had found means to quit Toulon, and had effected his escape with Miss Carmelite de Brissac, with success.

Half-an-hour later, to his astonishment, he saw the viscount crossing the yard. He made a sign—Pierre Berbins was by his side instantly, but D'Évreux did not speak. He led the way to the officers' quarters, and when they had gained his room he closed the door carefully.

' What has happened ? ' asked Pierre, whose curiosity was stimulated to its highest extent.

' An order was issued yesterday evening, signed by Barras, that no boat was, on any account, to be suffered to leave the harbour without a permit.'

' That is bad,' said the sergeant gnawing his thumb.

' I passed the whole night in looking for fishermen or sailors whom a bribe would induce to venture to put to sea. I could not find one ; at last I was regarded with considerable suspicion, and to make the matter worse, this morning I met Nicholas and Jean Poyer, arm-in-arm together.'

' Worse and worse ! ' cried Pierre Berbins.

' They are furious against you, if I may judge from what they let fall as they walked past. Jean did not find Nicholas at the cabaret you mentioned, and he thinks you were making fun of him ; Nicholas has been again to Miss de Brissac's late lodging, and is much annoyed to find her gone ; everything looks as black as possible for us. The aspect of affairs could not be more gloomy.'

Berbins groaned in anguish of spirit, he already saw three heads in the basket of the guillotine—his own, D'Evreux's, and Carmélite's.

' I can see nothing for it, but to go at once to Barras,' continued D'Evreux.

'To him! to the representative of the people! to Barras,' cried Berbins in astonishment.

'Yes! to the fountain head. I have hit upon a scheme which will I think be successful; desperate diseases require desperate remedies. Those ruffians must be baulked of their prey. If they find Miss de Brissac she will be executed, nothing can save her; we must act at once, am I not right?'

'Perfectly, but how to proceed?'

'I will tell you.'

The captain and his sergeant looked earnestly at one another.

CHAPTER V.

THE MARRIAGE WITH CARMELITE.

'As Nicholas knows where Miss de Brissac was concealed,' the Captain D'Evreux went on, 'he has but to make inquiries at the lodging-house, to find that she left in my company. That will give a clue which will probably lead to her discovery. We are all in danger'

'But Barras has given the lady's life to Jean,' said the sergeant.

'Yes, and yours to Nicholas! No matter! I will represent to him how odious it is for this sailor to pursue her as he does. In fact, I have my plan, await my return. I go to Barras.'

Leaving Berbins in amaze, D'Evreux sought an interview with the representative of the people, one of whose distinguishing characteristics was a clear and vigorous memory for even the minutest details.

No sooner did the captain mention the name of Miss de Brissac, than he recollected the whole affair, and agreed with D'Evreux that Jean Poyer's behaviour was to be strongly condemned.

'But what will you have, citizen captain?' he continued. 'He is a good patriot, and she belongs to a proscribed family. She is an aristocrat—her father is a traitor to the republic.'

'I have come more on behalf of the sergeant Berbins, who is in my company, than for the lady herself,' remarked D'Evreux.

'What interest can the soldier take in her?' asked Barras.

'I believe he is in love with her.'

'That may be, yet it is unpardonable for a soldier to screen an aristocrat. I fear they ought both to be sent to the guillotine,' said the representative of the people with a frown.

'But suppose, citizen,' replied D'Evreux, 'that she loses the taint of the aristocracy which at present clings to her and proves herself a good patriot by marrying a republican soldier?'

'To that I have no objection,' Barras replied. 'It is a good way of solving the difficulty and saving the life of a good soldier. I will consider the matter as settled. Let Miss de Brissac marry Sergeant Berbins in four and twenty hours and their lives shall be saved.'

'In spite of the patriots of the "Aristides."'

'You have my word, citizen, it is enough,' said Barras, waving his hand to intimate that the interview was over.

Captain the Viscount D'Evreux hastened back to the barracks, and recounted the conversation which had taken place between himself and the representative of people to Berbins, who, if he was amazed before, was now literally astounded.

'Marry me!' cried the sergeant; 'Miss de Brissac marry a man in my position when she is already engaged to you?'

'I don't mean seriously that she is to marry you,' answered D'Evreux, with an angry glance. 'Have you taken leave of your senses?'

'I believe I have within the last five minutes,' the sergeant replied.

'Listen to me. To marry Miss de Brissac is merely a subterfuge to save her. I can devise no other means, can you?'

' No,' said Berbins, with a melancholy shake of the head.

' Would you consign her to the guillotine—would you consign the three of us? If you can suggest anything better, I will be guided by you.'

Captain D'Evreux looked at him, but he remained silent.

' She will be your wife. I will undertake to gain her consent to that, though you will see nothing of her after she leaves the church, and you quit her side at the door of her lodgings. No one can demand the head of the *citoyenne*, Berbins, the wife of the brave patriot, Pierre Berbins. In a few days I hope to be able to fly with her to Germany, and you will have no difficulty in octaining a divorce, which every one will say is your right.'

' But consider.'

' What? ' anxiously asked D'Evreux.

' Shall I not cover myself with a shame, which to me has no real existence, but to the world at large, who do not know our arrangement.'

' Ridiculous scruple ! '

' I think not. When I do really marry, my wife will of course hear all about my first marriage. She will say his first wife deceived him and eloped with an officer; that is what it comes to, and perhaps the second may follow the example of the first.'

Captain D'Evreux bit his lips and appeared much embarrassed.

' She shall go away to Germany by herself; I will follow afterwards,' he said, suddenly.

' That is better ; yet——'

' Say no more! ' cried the captain, angrily; ' we will take our chance of the guillotine, from which you have no more chance of escaping than we, though I did expect that you would oblige me in this instance.'

'An authorisation is necessary for a soldier to marry,' said Berbins, still doubtful.

'Barras is to send it to my quarters. There will be no difficulty about the ceremony. Consent, my dear Berbins, and you will find us eternally grateful; you commenced the good work by saving Miss de Brissac from Jean Poyer; end it by saving her a second time. Jean is as merciless as a tiger, and your life is in the hands of Nicholas, who will be equally pitiless.'

'I consent,' answered Sergeant Berbins; 'after all it is a good action and must bring its reward. Arrange everything as you wish it, I will obey you as if on parade, captain.'

D'Evreux shook his hand heartily.

'You are a fine fellow,' he said, 'come with me. We must see Miss de Brissac at once, and make the necessary arrangements for the marriage.'

A short walk brought them to Carmélite's lodgings. She threw herself into her lover's arms and imprinted a kiss upon his lips.

'You have come at last,' she said, with a sigh. 'Oh, if you knew how long the time is while I am alone! all is so dreary, so blank, so hopeless! Ah!' she started on beholding Berbins, 'you have a stranger with you.'

'Not quite a stranger,' replied the captain, with a smile.

'Oh, no; it is my deliverer! I am glad you have brought him with you. It is everything to have a friend on whom you can rely in these dreadful times. Will you not sit down, my friend? we have no secrets that you may not hear.'

'He will take care of himself, Carmélite,' said D'Evreux; 'hear what I have to tell you.'

He related his interview with Barras and the scheme for her deliverance and ultimate safety, which they had adopted. When she had heard all, she went to Pierre, covered with blushes, but radiant with hope, thinking that her perils were over now.

' Will you really do this for me? ' she continued, in sweet confusion. ' How good of you—how can I ever thank you! I shall indeed have one regret, and that is, I am already engaged, and that my heart cannot go with my hand. It is seldom one meets with so disinterested and generous a man as you have shown yourself to be.'

Pierre tried to find a suitable answer for the lovely girl, but failed signally, and could only wipe a tear from his eye.

' Happier days are in store for France, I firmly believe,' exclaimed D'Evreux, ' and then we will think of Berbins. In the meantime, as far as money goes, I——'

' I want no pay,' interrupted the sergeant, finding his tongue. ' I am sufficiently rewarded by the kind way in which Miss Carmélite speaks ; and now the matter being settled, viscount, I will await your further orders in barracks.'

He saluted and retired, having the delicacy to leave the lovers together.

Carmélite de Brissac saw the necessity for the plan to be adopted. She did not hesitate to place herself in the power of a soldier in a marching regiment, to save her life. She believed in his honour and his devotion to his superior officer, and freely allowed D'Evreux to make any preparations he pleased.

She looked forward to being in a few days on the road to Spain or Germany, where her lover would join her, and in a month at the latest she expected to be with her father and the Bishop D'Arvilliers, and to see such of her friends as had escaped the fury of the Republicans, and the murderous edge of the guillotine.

In 1793, in a town like Toulon, which had just been taken possession of by a section of the national army, military force, to some extent, superseded civil rule.

There was nothing very extraordinary in permission being given by one of the proconsuls of the convention to a Republican soldier to marry a lady of rank whose father had fled. It was considered a very proper chastisement, one calculated to reduce her pride, and prove to her the efficacy of equality.

During the day the marriage was registered at the office of the municipality, and Miss Carmélite de Brissac became legally the wife of Pierre Berbins.

The religious ceremony followed early in the morning of the next day. As Pierre stood by Carmélite's side in the church, he thought he had never seen so pretty and engaging a girl as his pretended wife; he began to wish, in fact, that she was his in reality. The dawn of love broke in his heart—a love which he felt was disgraceful to him, and which he must check at all hazards. Still it existed, and he wondered he had not suspected its existence before.

When he left the church, with her still by his side for the sake of appearance, he would have given ten years of his life for one kiss from the lips of the woman who was by law his wife. She was pale and pre-occupied, but neither tearful or melancholy. She did not speak as they walked back to the lodgings where Captain D'Evreux was awaiting her coming. Yet Berbins knew she was happy in the prospect of the future and he was satisfied. At the door he made a respectful bow, and said, though his voice trembled slightly—

'I have the honour to wish you good-day, miss.'

'Thank you very, very much,' answered Carmélite, enthusiastically.

She extended her hand, he grasped it, he raised it to his lips, and the next instant, turning round, he was walking stiffly back to barracks, as if with his company on parade.

And this was how Miss Carmélite de Brissac was married.

CHAPTER VI.

DARKEST HOUR JUST BEFORE DAWN.

SOME days elapsed and Carmélite saw nothing of her husband. She began to grow alarmed. It had been arranged between them that he should make preparations immediately for their flight to Coblentz, where numerous proscribed friends of theirs had taken refuge; he would have, in adopting this step, to give up his position in the French army, but his sentiments had never been with the Republicans. He was a loyalist and an aristocrat, having served with the army in order to preserve his life, so that he was at heart glad of a chance to escape from a state of things of which he disapproved.

On the evening of the third day she received a visit from Pierre Berbins.

'You have come from the viscount!' she exclaimed, seizing his hand.

'Alas! no, miss,' he answered.

His face was very grave, and her heart sank within her as she read there evil tidings.

'If anything has happened, I implore you to tell me at once,' she continued; 'anything is preferable to this suspense.'

'It is best that she should know it,' remarked the sergeant as if speaking to himself.

'Oh, yes. I am brave. See, I am strong and calm,' said the heroic girl, striving to appear so.

'The Viscount D'Évreux is dead,' exclaimed Sergeant Berbins.

'Dead! Oh, heaven pity me!' cried Carmélite, sinking back into a chair, pale as a ghost, and trembling violently all over.

Berbins thought she was going to swoon, but she did not faint, her agony was too acute for that; she waited to hear more.

'He was denounced as an aristocrat by Jean Poyer, the sailor of the "Aristides." Letters from your father and the able D'Arvilliers were found upon him, and after a lengthened trial he was condemned and shot as a traitor to the Republic.'

'This is dreadful,' murmured Carmélite. 'Dead? D'Evreux dead? What charms has life for me?'

Seeing that she was overwhelmed with grief, the sergeant did not speak for some time.

'Did he send no message to me?' she asked.

'His last words were of you,' answered the sergeant.

'Tell me them.'

'He said, "Berbins, give her my undying love, and add that it is my wish that she should try to become a Republican. The days of monarchy and aristocracy are gone for ever. She will live safely if she decides upon being in reality your wife as she is already legally. This is my last wish. You are my friend. I should like my Carmélite to be my friend's wife."'

'He said that?' cried Carmélite.

'Truly.'

'And you have the insolence to repeat such a proposal to me. Monsieur, the blood of all the Brissacs rises up in my veins and forbids such a profanation. You may lead me to the scaffold. I will go to death as bravely as did the Viscount D'Evreux, for let me tell you that I infinitely prefer death to dishonour.'

She was superior to her grief as she said this, and stood like Niobe all tears, but yet firm and resolved.

Sergeant Berbins shrank back in affright. Her

grandeur subdued him, but at the same time excited his admiration and stimulated his passion, for in reality he had conceived a sincere and maddening love for the beautiful girl.

'Pardon me, ma'm'selle,' he stammered.

'Monsieur, I cannot pardon you,' she replied with dignity. 'If my beloved friend in his last moments so far forgot himself and what was owing to me as to entrust such a message to you, I am sorry. When the angel of death is hovering over us, our minds may not be so strong as at other times, but for you there is no excuse, no pardon. You come here soberly and rationally to insult me, and at the supreme moment of my bereavement.'

'But if ma'am'selle will consider ——'

'I have done so, monsieur, and you have unpardonably offended me; I tell you so plainly, whatever the consequences of your resentment may be. Go, if you please—leave me!'

'Have I no right here?' demanded the sergeant, becoming braver.

'Oh, monsieur,' exclaimed Carmélite, with a smile which, in its satiric force, cut him to the quick, 'if you presume upon your strength and your legal position to insult me still further, I have only one thing to say.'

'And that is— ?'

'I have concealed in the body of my dress a poignard and with that I am prepared to protect my honour.'

Berbins was completely baffled. He fell back and knew not what to say.

Seeing her advantage, Carmélite continued, 'What I should have expected from a man who has, up to this day, behaved as you have done, is far different from what has occurred.'

'Will mademoiselle be good enough to explain?' said the sergeant.

' You should now offer to conduct me through your lines, and place before me the means of reaching Germany. To you the task would not be difficult.'

' Your object in going to Germany ? '

' Monsieur is impertinent.'

' Not at all. Believe me, more depends upon your answer than you imagine. I beg mademoiselle to inform me.'

' My life is blighted,' said Carmélite, the tears again starting to her eyes ; ' I wish to place myself with my friends, and so communicate with my relations. Then I shall enter a convent, and end my days in the service of my Creator. Is monsieur satisfied ? '

' Perfectly. I entreat your forgiveness. You shall not be mistaken in me. Be pleased to dress yourself, and I will at once conduct you beyond our lines, and— and all will be well.'

Sergeant Berbins spoke with difficulty, but Carmélite was only too glad of the opportunity of escaping. She took him at his word, not noticing his confusion, or suspecting that anything was concealed under his manner. In a short time she was dressed and ready for the journey. She had money. Berbins was overwhelmed by her with thanks and protestations of gratitude, but he only smiled grimly, and appeared to resemble a man who is experiencing the pleasure of doing a good action.

They walked through the town without molestation, not even taking the trouble to pursue the bye streets. In a frequented thoroughfare they met Jean Poyer, who, grating his teeth, said, ' There goes the citizen soldier with his bride. Ha, ha, Citizen Brissac, I am revenged at last !' and he and his associates laughed aloud.

Carmélite clung closer to her preserver for protection from these wild men, and he endeavoured to reassure

her, apologising as opportunity presented itself for his
conduct a few minutes before.

At last he got her to a small house at the extremity
of the city, and there she found a chaise, with two
horses, waiting.

'This is for you, mademoiselle,' exclaimed the sergeant.

'For me?'

'Yes; ask no questions, please. Go to the driver
and say "Thormidos," he will reply "Brumaire," and
all will be well. Mademoiselle will sometimes think of
me.'

'Ever with gratitude,' answered Carmélite, shaking
his hand cordially.

The next instant Sergeant Berbins was gone, and in
the darkness he wiped away a tear from his eye.

Carmélite advanced like one in a dream.

In a timid voice she said 'Thormidos.'

Before she could recover from her astonishment she
found herself clasped in the arms of a man who sprang
from the carriage. He covered her with kisses—he
called her by her name.

It was the Viscount D'Evreux.

'You darling!' she murmured. 'Can this be real?'

'Why not, my sweet one?' answered the young
officer's cheerful voice. 'I have been planning this for
days past. Did not Berbins tell you?'

'Ye-es,' she stammered.

Sergeant Berbins had behaved nobly after all. If he
tried to gain her for himself by the invention of a subterfuge it was because the poor fellow loved her, and
she resolved that D'Evreux should never learn from
her the particulars of his attempted treachery.

Time was precious as D'Evreux hurried her into
the chaise, which immediately started.

Carmelite was almost delirious with joy; her lover,

whom she thought dead, overwhelmed her with caresses. After night came the bright morn. It was worth while to suffer if awakening to the truth could be so delightful.

They made their escape to Germany, and were afterwards married at Coblentz. Sergeant Berbins was handsomely rewarded by Carmelite's friends in happier times, and in his breast and that of Miss de Brissac's was locked the secret of his temptation, and the falsehood to which it gave birth, for which, however, he had afterwards handsomely atoned.

A MATCH-MAKING MOTHER.

FRIGID, ice-bound winter had just given place to fresh and balmy spring. The grateful earth was preparing to bring forth its increase; the lambs frolicked in the fields; the mavis whistled cheerily amid the green leaves of the monarch oaks; Nature threw off her lethargy, and all things animate and inanimate bowed down before the mighty life-giver, whose rays gladdened creation, and made the heart of man rejoice.

Yet was there mourning.

A noble mansion situated in the heart of a midland county had just yielded up its dead.

Stanforth Harrington, a man of large property, slept in the family vault, leaving his wife and daughter to lament his loss.

Colonel Harrington had held a commission in the rifle brigade, but retired from the service when an estate became his by the death of his father. This estate, however, was strictly entailed, and, in default of heirs male, passed away from him and went into the hands of a distant relation.

The colonel died young; but he had always led a hard life. The want of a son and heir also affected him, and made him more reckless of his health and fortune than he otherwise would have been.

It must not, however, be supposed that Colonel Harrington left his wife and daughter totally unprovided for.

On the contrary, his life had been heavily insured in more than one office, and he had private property of his own which was absolutely his wife's at his death.

When this melancholy event occurred, Beatrice Harrington was a little more than seventeen years of age.

Hers was not the fashionable style of beauty at the present day, though she was undeniably lovely.

Her eyes were full and lustrous, flashing with a subtle fire : her hair dark as a raven's plume ; but her complexion delicately white, like polished ivory. Her features were of that much-coveted Grecian type, which imparts such an air of dignified grace to its possessor ; her mouth and ears were small, as were her almost Lilliputian hands and feet. In stature she was below, rather than above, the average height.

When she chose, a sweet, ravishing smile stole over her face, giving her commanding beauty a power which it was difficult to withstand.

When Beatrice fancied herself unobserved, a pensive loveliness took possession of her, which made her, in the opinion of some, still more fascinating.

Mrs. Harrington and her daughter were painfully aware that they would be compelled in a short time to quit the house which had been a cherished home to them for many years.

The heir-at-law had, through his solicitor, written them a peremptory letter, informing them that he should expect the premises to be vacated within a given time.

Rather glad to quit a house which now contained nothing for them but gloomy associations, unlightened by one gleam of hope in the future, they expedited their departure rather than delayed it, and sought relief in the whirl and bustle of London.

Fearing to incur the inevitable expense of an hotel

until the financial condition of their affairs was accurately ascertained, they took up their abode in modest lodgings in the neighbourhood of Bayswater.

Here they were speedily visited by Mr. Burt, the family attorney, a gentleman who had conducted the legal business of Colonel Harrington for a considerable period of time.

Mr. Burt was growing old. He had long ago virtually given up his business to his two sons, though it was still his pride and delight to wander every day over the office, and pretend to conduct the various cases that were entrusted to the management of the firm.

In the present instance he had stolen a march upon his eldest son, and having gained what may be called surreptitious information, walked from Lincoln's-inn to Bayswater to let Mrs. Harrington know what her income really was to be during her widowhood.

There were two shops in Oxford Street that little Mr. Burt had a weakness for; one was a tobacconist's, whose window had a large sheet of looking-glass in it which enabled the lawyer to see if his frilled shirt was unruffled, and if his hat was placed jauntily on one side, as became a gay old gentleman who had not forgotten how to look slily at a pretty girl when he passed her in the street.

The other was a hairdresser's shop, the front of which was adorned with the head and shoulders of a lady in wax who revolved upon a pedestal, now turning her rouged cheeks and cherry-tinted lips to the spectator, anon revealing the immaculate purity of her alabaster neck and the wondrous parting of her back hair.

Mr. Burt would stand until the policeman on the beat regarded him suspiciously looking at this mimic fair one. He ardently wished that kind fate would treat him as if he were a second Pygmalion, as he would gladly have passed the remainder of his life in worshipping his mute ideal. It was a wonder he did not summon her to show cause why she wasn't real.

At length he reached Bayswater, and found the ladies dressed in deep mourning. They were glad to see him, and treated him as an old friend.

After the usual courtesies had been exchanged, **Mrs.** Harrington exclaimed—

' You will, I know, Mr. Burt, excuse my anxiety to know what provision the colonel has made for us. Of course we are fully aware that our circumstances have greatly changed since my poor husband's death.'

' They have,' returned Mr. Burt, pulling up his shirt frill. ' But though I have to all intents and purposes retired from the business, yet I made it my task to obtain the information required by the wife of my old friend and patron.'

' That is very good of you, I am sure,' said **Mrs.** Harrington, scarcely able to conceal her impatience.

' We find that you will have, when all claims upon the colonel are settled, an annual income of seven hundred pounds.'

' And that is all ? ' ejaculated Mrs. Harrington.

It was not much.

Accustomed as she had been from her earliest infancy to luxuries of every description, and to a superfluity rather than a dearth of money, she felt very acutely this radical change in her position.

Although not allied by birth to the aristocracy, **Mrs.** Harrington belonged to a rich City family ; but shortly after her marriage one of those periodical crises arrived which scattered the wealth of her friends, and destroyed both her own and her husband's expectations in that quarter.

After delivering his news, Mr. Burt took a glass of wine and his leave, walking back the way he came, standing in mute adoration before his idol, and surveying his insignificant person in the reflecting glass which had been placed there by the spirited proprietor for a very different purpose.

Turning to her daughter, Mrs. Harrington said—

'Now that we know what we have to depend upon, we must look matters in the face.'

'I'm sure I don't want much, mamma,' replied Beatrice.

'Don't talk nonsense, child; you want everything. It is your wants which trouble me.'

'How can that be?' asked Beatrice, in undisguised surprise.

'Because I can do nothing without you. It is to you that I look to make a good marriage which will restore me to the position we have lost through that unlucky entail.'

'Oh, mamma!' exclaimed Beatrice, much shocked, 'what a time to talk of marriage!'

And she looked deprecatingly from her black dress to her mother.

'I know it,' replied Mrs. Harrington; 'and I know that we can do nothing for twelve months. The ways of society will condemn me to that period of inactivity. It has occurred to me that the most sensible thing to do will be to accept the invitation sent us by your maiden aunt, my sister, and visit her at Torquay for a few months. While there you can perfect yourself in German, Italian, and Spanish, and cultivate those musical tastes which you possess in so marked a degree.'

'After that?'

'We must not anticipate, but it is more than probable that I shall plan a continental tour.

The invitation was accepted. The few months extended themselves into twelve, and it was exactly a year before the Harringtons left the hospitable roof of the maiden aunt.

When Mrs. Harrington found that nothing but a prudent and wealthy match on the part of her daughter could restore them to anything like their former position, she never lost an opportunity of instilling worldly lessons into her mind ; but she did not find her such an apt pupil as she could have wished.

Beatrice longed, as every true woman does, for a loving heart which she could call her own, and which she knew pulsed lovingly for her every minute of the day and night.

Love, even if it were with poverty as a companion ; love shaded by misery ; love hand in hand with alienation from parent, home, friends.

Such was her dream.

When Mrs. Harrington left her sister's house, she proceeded to London, and expended a large sum of money in providing her daughter and herself with a wardrobe of most fashionable and expensive dresses.

' Dress, my child,' she observed, ' is everything. A woman badly dressed, even if she be beautiful as Venus, is thrown away. To dazzle, you must dress with perfect taste and costly materials ; taste for the men, costliness for the women. It is a clever woman's endeavour to be envied by the latter, and admired by the former at all hazards.

Whereat Beatrice opened her eyes.

They determined to proceed to the Continent. Spring had come again, and the Paris season was at its height when that of London was just beginning.

Mrs. Harrington armed herself with a few good introductions and started for Dover, where she stayed a few days, observing that there were occasionally some good people to be met with at Dover.

It will be observed by the attentive reader that this valuable mother never threw a chance away.

They took up their temporary abode at the Lord

Warden, that being acknowledged the best hotel in the place, and Mrs. Harrington set herself to find out who was staying in the house.

' Positively no one, my dear,' she exclaimed, as she returned from an inspection of the list. ' Not a soul who is anybody ; a few tradesmen and parvenues, a sprinkling of commercials, a few army men, and *voilà tout.*'

' How tiresome ! ' observed Beatrice, not caring at all about the matter, but willing to sympathise with her mother in her evident distress.

' Oh, I must leave to-morrow,' continued Mrs. Harrington ; ' I can never afford to waste money in such a barren spot as this.'

' When you like,' said Beatrice, with a sigh.

' Ah ! you are right to sigh,' cried her mother ; ' but wait—wait until we cross the Channel, then you shall see beauty, wealth, rank, and talent, I promise you.'

In the afternoon they walked on the Parade. The wind was rather high, and Beatrice would have lost her hat several times, had she not taken the precaution to confine it with a piece of elastic.

Suddenly her mother pinched her arm severely.

' Oh ! ' ejaculated Beatrice, at a loss to account for such strange behaviour.

' Let your hat fall,' exclaimed Mrs. Harrington.

' Why ? '

' Never mind, do as I tell you,' was the only response her mother condescended to give her.

Beatrice did as she was bid, and her hat rolled gaily along the stones, past a couple of gaily-dressed girls, until it brushed against the legs of a gentleman, who made a snatch at it, missed it, and ran after it for some distance, not desisting until he caught it.

Then he looked round for its owner.

Beatrice at once suggested herself ; Beatrice, with

her lovely hair streaming in the breeze, and looking the picture of loveliness in distress.

Advancing towards her, he exclaimed—

'Pardon me, but I think I have been fortunate enough to recover your hat.'

'Yes, thank you,' said Beatrice, lowering her eyes, modestly.

The man who stood before her was a tall, gentlemanly fellow, about five-and-thirty years of age. His manner was bold and defiant, his demeanour singularly polite; but upon his face sat an expression of dissipation and sensual indulgence as plainly to be read by a practised eye as if it had been engraved upon his massive brow.

'Oh, you are too good,' Mrs. Harrington hastened to chime in; 'my poor Beatrice is so careless. She will not take pains. It is quite a charity to scold her sometimes.'

'I am sure that so charming a young lady cannot stand in need of scolding,' said the gentleman, smiling.

'May we know to whom we are indebted for such unexpected kindness?' continued Mrs. Harrington, in her most persuasive and insinuating manner.

'I am Sir Frederick Cazenove,' he answered.

'Thanks very much, Sir Frederick, for your amiability. We stop a week more in Dover; may we hope to have the pleasure of a visit? I think I have heard my late husband, Colonel Harrington, speak of you; and any friend of his will be of course doubly welcome.'

'I do not know the name; but I shall esteem it an honour to call,' answered Sir Frederick.

So saying, he raised his hat and passed on as Mrs. Harrington gave him a nod of adieu.

'Who is he, mamma?' asked Beatrice, when they had gone a little way.

' Did you not hear him say he was Sir Frederick Cazenove ? '

' And did papa ever speak of him ? '

' No, you simpleton; that was a device of mine to make his acquaintance.   I knew he was a man of some celebrity, because I saw him come from that yacht lying in the harbour.'

' When ? '

' My dear, you are not nearly observant enough; you are not, indeed.   He landed in a small boat ten minutes back.'

When the mother and daughter returned to the hotel Mrs. Harrington inquired respecting Sir Frederick Cazenove.

She was informed by a garrulous waiter, a native of Dover, that Sir Frederick resided at the Hermitage, a few miles inland; that he had at least fifteen thousand a year; that he was very fond of yachting, spent much of his time abroad, and was considered rather eccentric by the good, sober, honesty-loving people of Dover.

' Excellent ! ' remarked Mrs. Harrington, as she recapitulated all this to her daughter.   ' But, dear me, I forgot to tell him where we were staying.   Still, he cannot make a mistake.   We did not look like a second-rate hotel, did we, my dear? '

' I hope not, mamma,' replied Beatrice.

Mrs. Harrington devoutly echoed this wish.

' And so we stop here another week ? ' said Beatrice.

' Of course; there is a chance.'

' Of what ? '

' Wait, my child,' replied Mrs. Harrington, oracularly; ' see what the future will bring forth.   It is bad to count your chickens before they are hatched, however good an incubator your hen may be.'

Beatrice sighed again.

She wondered whether the peace she longed for would ever be hers.

Looking out of the window she saw Sir Frederick Cazenove's yacht, the ' Phryne,' lying at anchor.

' I should like to have a yacht!' she exclaimed involuntarily.

' That rests entirely with you,' replied her mother, who had overheard her remark.

Beatrice cast down her eyes in confusion.

She knew to what her mother alluded.

.   .   .   .   .

The waiter at the Lord Warden did not exaggerate in the least when he described Sir Frederick Cazenove as eccentric.

He was, indeed, a notorious libertine.

Those who knew him related stories of which he was the hero—stories which made the blood run chill and the flesh creep as the speakers spoke with bated breath.

And yet in appearance he was mild, amiable, and gentlemanly in the extreme. It was only in his eye that the devil lurked.

His yacht, a magnificent triumph of the ship-builder's art, lay in the basin inside the harbour. On board were the captain, and Bowker, the mate. The two sailors who completed the complement of the vessel were on shore.

Captain Hicks was entirely a creature of Sir Frederick's. He had been saved from a great danger by the baronet, and ever since he had attached himself to his preserver with extraordinary fidelity.

The history of Bowker was somewhat different.

Sir Frederick always preferred to have about him men who were either bound to him by gratitude or compelled to serve him through fear.

The latter was Bowker's case.

Sir Frederick was spending a few days at his seat near Dover, the Hermitage. In the middle of the night he was aroused by a noise as of a man breaking into the house. Seizing a pistol, he went to the spot from whence the noise proceeded, and seeing a man in the act of decamping with a large parcel of valuable property, shot him in the leg, and brought him to the ground like a winged pheasant.

Finding that the fellow was harmless, he summoned his valet, a man of the name of Abel Smith, who was the depository of many of his master's secrets.

'This man,' he exclaimed, 'came to visit me, Smith, but as he did not announce himself, he met with an accident, and I fancy he is badly hurt. Look to him, will you?'

Smith knelt down on the carpet, and by the aid of a flickering candle examined the man's wound.

'I'll tie it up for to-night, sir, but he will require a doctor in the morning. The bullet has entered his thigh and lodged there.'

'It has lodged where it is likely to stay until daylight,' said Sir Frederick, with a laugh. 'Take his heels while I take his head, and let us put him out of sight somewhere.'

They carried him to a bedroom in an unfrequented part of the house, and there left him groaning terribly.

A villainous countenance had the man. There was nothing intellectual about him. Strength he had, like all other brutes, but his ferocity was his chief characteristic.

He could not understand the clemency of which he was the object.

'Oh,' thought he, 'they will take me to gaol in the morning. It was too late to do so when that cursed shot rolled me over like a dog on the carpet.'

In spite of the pain of his wound he got off to sleep

after a time, and did not wake until the doctor roused him.

When the bullet was extracted the man felt very faint from loss of blood, and some of his native ferocity had evaporated.

Sir Frederick came to see him. The wounded man's eyes glistened as he made his appearance.

'What's your name?' asked Sir Frederick.

'Bowker,' was the sullen reply.

'Listen to me, Bowker,' continued the baronet. 'It is in my power to hand you over to the police. Were I to do so you would languish in prison for a considerable period; but I will consider your wound a sufficient punishment on one condition.'

'What's that, master?' inquired Bowker, regarding him earnestly from beneath his shaggy brows.

'You must exchange one sort of servitude for another. You must be mine, body and soul; dare to disobey me, and I hand you over to your doom.'

The man hesitated.

'I—I'd rather take my chance,' he said.

'Think; the choice rests with you. Good food, liberal wages, coupled with implicit obedience on the one hand; imprisonment, hard labour—'

'I know it all. I've been through it, and rather than do it again, I'm yours.'

This sealed Bowker's fate.

When his wound was healed he was put on board the yacht, and he had been Captain Hick's attendant ever since.

Bowker was a gloomy, discontented, surly wretch. He had never been married. He had neither friends or relations, being a foundling and a parish brat. The only thing that he ever attached himself to, or that ever attached itself to him, was a huge, savage-looking dog of the mastiff breed.

Rasper was always at Bowker's side, and the rough, beetle-browed man loved him with a wild passionate fondness which was the only indication of his possessing a heart.

As for Rasper, he was miserable if he let his master out of his sight.

On the afternoon of the day upon which Mrs. Harrington so cleverly made the acquaintance of Sir Frederick Cazenove, Captain Hicks had left Bowker and his dog in charge of the 'Phyrne.'

Hicks felt, as he phrased it, 'a little spreeish,' so he went on shore, and indulged in several libations with doubtful females in various taverns and pot-houses.

When he returned to the yacht, about six o'clock, he was rather unsteady about his legs, and had an irresistible inclination to sway about from one side to the other.

It was a little hazy, and Bowker had lighted a fire on deck in a brazier, which flamed and flared without shedding much light upon surrounding objects.

As the shades of night were falling, Sir Frederick Cazenove came on board.

' Hicks, Hicks!' he shouted down the companion.

' Ay, ay, sir,' responded the captain.

' Oh, you're there. All right. Stop a minute, I'll come down to you.'

In a few seconds he was in the cabin.

' Will you try a drop of our grog, Sir Frederick?' asked Hicks; 'it's none of your three-water.'

' Not now,' replied Sir Frederick, removing the cigar from his mouth while he spoke; 'I came to put a few questions to you. First of all, how are the stores?'

' Not perfect, sir, though pretty nearly so.'

' Are we ready to put to sea at a moment's notice?'

' No, sir.'

'It is as I thought. See to it. In a day or two I may wish to up anchor, and set sail for the Mediterranean. The ladies' cabin,' added Sir Frederick, 'how is that?'

'Just as you left it, sir, when——'

'Oh, it has not been used since that occasion, eh? Well, you must put it in order. Get the yacht in proper trim ; when you want money come to me. See to it all. I rely upon you.'

'Very well, sir, it shall be attended to,' responded Hicks, respectfully.

When the baronet had taken his departure, the men looked at one another.

'The governor's after another petticoat,' exclaimed Captain Hicks.

'He's wonderful at that sort of game,' said Bowker. 'It's all change with him. He can never stop in one place a month. Something new is what he spends his life in hunting after.'

'There's something in the wind, that you may take your oath, and we'd better have all taut in case of squalls.'

When he was alone in his berth that night, Bowker soliloquised—an unusual thing for him—

'Poor thing! I wonder who she is. She little guesses what's in store for her. There was the last— how I pitied her! never shall I get that sight out of my eyes. Her screams seem to ring in my ears still. If I could help myself; but I am bound hand and foot ; no slave was ever more securely held in bondage. God help his next victim?'

Sir Frederick Cazenove did not fail to keep his appointment with the Harringtons ; the ensuing day did not elapse without his calling at the Lord Warden and asking for the ladies with whom he had accidentally become acquainted on the Parade.

Mrs. Harrington was at home, so was Beatrice. The latter had been especially desirous of going out after lunch, but her mother would not allow her.

'He is sure to call,' she said, 'and I would not have you miss him for the world.'

Sir Frederick Cazenove, the very pink of fashion, entered the drawing-room after the waiter, who announced him in a loud tone of voice, as if he felt it an honour to pronounce his name.

'You see, Mrs. Harrington,' said Sir Frederick, with a bland smile, 'that I have lost no time in accepting your invitation.'

'It gives me great pleasure to see you,' she replied. 'Pray take a seat.'

Sir Frederick sat down between the mother and daughter, but nearest to the latter.

'Do you stay long in Dover?' he asked.

'Really, I scarcely know; our movements are so uncertain. We are free as air, and having no encumbrances can go where we like.'

'That is precisely my case,' remarked the baronet.

'How very agreeable! And are you fond of travelling?'

'Adore it! And you?'

'It has been my sole ambition all my life. Dear Beatrice here has such a longing to see Switzerland.'

'"Where Alps on Alps arise,"' quoted the baronet.

'Ah! you are poetical? But I need not ask that question; every man of taste and refinement must be so.'

'I had a reason in asking you if you were about to stay long at Dover,' continued Sir Frederick.

'Indeed!'

'The fact is, I ransacked my memory last night, and I find that I was intimately acquainted at one time with Colonel Harrington of the—the—'

' 60th Rifles,' suggested the relict of that gallant officer.

' Thank you, yes. The name had escaped my memory at the time you spoke. Now, I should esteem it a favour if you would permit me to extend what little hospitality is in my power to the widow and daughter of so old a friend and worthy a gentleman.'

Mrs. Harrington raised the corner of her lace-edged handkerchief to her eye.

The kind and generous way in which Sir Frederick spoke had presumably affected her to tears.

' I trust I have not aroused any painful emotions,' Sir Frederick hastened to say.

' N—no,' replied Mrs. Harrington, with a half sob. ' But I am so very susceptible—my loss is so recent—he was so dear to me ! '

There was a pause.

Mrs. Harrington gradually recovered herself.

' May I flatter myself that my invitation will be accepted ? ' continued the baronet.

' For a few days ; I cannot promise to stay longer. Dear Beatrice is dying to reach Paris,' replied Mrs. Harrington.

' I will send my carriage for you to-morrow to bring you to the Hermitage ; that is arranged.'

' You are very kind,' returned Mrs. Harrington.

After some conversation on indifferent matters Sir Frederick took his leave.

Beatrice sat still and did not speak a word.

' How dull you are, Beaty ! ' said her mother; ' I consider it very unkind of you. Here do I take the greatest trouble for your sake, and the whole time Sir Frederick was here you would not open your mouth.'

' For my sake ? '

' Certainly. Is it not the wish nearest my heart to see you comfortably settled in life ? '

K

'There seemed something indecent to me, mamma, in the way you fished for an invitation,' replied Beatrice. 'If, as you say, you never heard the colonel speak of Sir Frederick, his declaration of intimacy must have been substantially false.'

'Of course. I knew that very well all the time. He has taken a fancy to you, and wishes to have us at his place, so that he can make love to you.'

'Any one would think I was an article of merchandise to be bought and sold,' said Beatrice, disdainfully.

'My dear child,' replied her mother gravely, 'people in our position cannot afford to throw chances away. Remember that.'

Beatrice was silent. It was useless to attempt to reason with her worldly mother.

Mrs. Harrington had her way, and when the carriage came the next day to convey them to the Hermitage they were in readiness.

The Hermitage was a large straggling house, situated in the midst of a handsome park, thickly timbered. The walls were for the most part covered with ivy. Rooks, wood-pigeons, starlings, and sparrows abounded. It was the *beau idéal* of an old romantic dwelling.

Beatrice shuddered as she beheld it, but her mother was enraptured with it.

'Oh, what a dear old place!' she exclaimed. 'I think I could give the world for such a house.'

'If it isn't haunted I am much mistaken,' rejoined Beatrice. 'Those rooms up there, under the tower, have an air which speaks volumes, and tells me they are peopled with ghosts.'

'Don't be so absurd!' said her mother, angrily. 'A girl educated as you have been should know better than to indulge such silly fancies.'

'I shall not be easy an hour while I am here,' continued Beatrice. 'Look at that wing, mamma. Do you notice that the blinds are all pulled down, just as if there was some one dead there?'

'It is disused, perhaps.'

The carriage now drove up. Sir Frederick stood on the step, waiting to receive them, and do the honours of his establishment in person.

He conducted them into the dining-room, which was handsomely furnished, though the furniture was all antique. Family and other portraits hung from the walls. A cold collation was served, to which he invited them to do justice.

They ate the wing of a chicken and drank a glass of wine apiece at his request, and were shown to their apartments by the housekeeper, an elderly female of singularly forbidding aspect.

The rooms set apart for the mother and daughter looked upon the lawn, and were in the centre of the house. Although they were replete with every comfort they also partook of the ghostly appearance which was everywhere so noticeable in this ancient mansion.

The heavy Arabian bedsteads shrouded in drapery, long, rich, and pall-like; the thick carpets into which the foot sank at every turn; the deep embrasures of the windows; the curious diamond-shaped panes of glass set in lead which those windows contained; the dull flapping of ivy leaves and branches against the panes; the sullen howl of the wind as it swept under the gables and tore round the chimney-tops; the massive oaken wardrobes and chairs, black with age; the huge fire-places and high mantel-pieces—combined with the tapestried walls to raise a sensation of awe in the mind of the beholder.

Beatrice shuddered a second time.

'What ails you, child?' asked her mother, when Mrs. Greaves, the housekeeper, had retired and left them to themselves.

K 2

'When I entered these rooms I felt a presentiment of coming evil. Oh, mamma! I may be very weak and nervous—I am willing to admit that I am a silly little fool—but I cannot divest my mind of the belief that there is danger lurking in the air.'

'Danger of what description?' asked Mrs. Harrington, regarding her with a puzzled look.

'Nay, that is more than I can tell.'

'Tut!' said Mrs. Harrington, unable to conceal an expression of great annoyance; 'you have been reading novels lately.'

Beatrice sat down in an arm-chair, and burst into tears.

Her mother did not attempt to comfort her, thinking it would be better to let her weep.

When Mrs. Harrington had changed her dress, Beatrice was still crying.

'If you are so foolish as to make your eyes red and swollen,' she exclaimed, 'I must leave you here until you recover yourself.'

'Oh, do not leave me!' cried Beatrice.

'Yes, it is fitting that you should be punished for your stupidity. Moreover, you will then have an opportunity of proving how ill-founded your suspicions are.'

In spite of her daughter's protestations, Mrs. Harrington left her to herself.

Beatrice, unable to remain alone, quickly changed her dress, dried her tears, and prepared to follow her mother.

But in her eagerness she mistook the way—a very easy achievement, by the way, in such an old-fashioned house—and instead of going towards the grand staircase proceeded along a corridor which led directly to the west wing.

This part of the house was that which Beatrice had

remarked on account of the blinds being drawn down externally, giving it the appearance of being uninhabited. That this was not the case, however, oil-lamps burning at intervals in the passage clearly proved.

When Beatrice came to the conviction that she had wandered in a wrong direction, she turned to retrace her steps.

Suddenly in the imperfect light she saw a door open, and beheld a pair of eyes brightly shining. Almost immediately the door was closed, and Beatrice went on with the impression that she had been favoured with a view of a woman's face.

'There is some mystery about this house,' she murmured. 'Oh, that I were out of it!'

By dint of perseverance she regained the grand staircase, and descended to the drawing-room, where Sir Frederick and her mother were engaged in friendly conversation.

A few days passed very agreeably, in spite of Beatrice's gloomy anticipations. They rode, drove, sketched, and yachted.

A ball was advertised to take place in Dover, in aid of some local charity, and Mrs. Harrington expressed a wish to go. It was accordingly arranged, and Sir Frederick purchased some tickets.

'I want him to see you in a low dress, Beaty,' said her mother. 'Girls are always so attractive in low dresses.'

As Beatrice was alighting from her carriage, a man standing on the pavement slipped a note into her hand.

She took it involuntarily, and the next minute was in the building in which the ball was held.

The man was Bowker.

While taking off her shawl, and drinking a cup of coffee, she glanced with a woman's curiosity at the note.

It ran as follows—

'Be particular which way the carriage drives to-night. If it goes to the westward, in the direction of Shakespeare's Cliff, there is danger ; refuse to proceed, and escape at all hazards.   A FRIEND.'

'Some one is joking with me,' she said to herself. 'It is a trick; but I will not be frightened.'

Certainly the Hermitage was on the eastern side; and if the carriage did bear to the west, it would be a remarkable coincidence.

While listening to the strains of the music and whirling in the giddy waltz, she forgot all about the mysterious warning, and laughed as heartily as the rest of them.

Sir Frederick Cazenove surpassed himself that evening to be agreeable to the ladies.

It was difficult to think anything bad of so amiable a man.

To a girl who has seen little of society balls are always the oases which render the Sahara of domestic life at all bearable.

Pretty, agile, untiring, conscious of admiration deservedly bestowed, she knows not fatigue, and dances, smiles, and chatters incessantly.

It was so with Beatrice.

She was in the humour to believe anything.

Sir Frederick Cazenove took her down to supper, purposely losing sight of Mrs. Harrington. A little sparkling wine, judiciously applied, made Beatrice still more deliciously careless and happy.

'Shall we join the dancers again?' asked Beatrice, panting for the ball-room, and seeing that some couples were already departing for the Terpsichorean arena.

'As you please,' he rejoined; 'I should, however, greatly prefer a lounge in the conservatory, and a short uninterrupted conversation with you.'

'With me!' exclaimed Beatrice, elevating her eyebrows in surprise.

They rose from the table and walked leisurely from the room. As they quitted it they met Mrs. Harrington leaning on the arm of an elderly gentleman in uniform extensively *decoré.* She smiled, and bowed graciously to Sir Frederick Cazenove and her daughter, and was evidently much pleased.

The baronet led his young and lovely partner into a long room, which had been fitted up as a conservatory, and was filled with numerous shrubs and flowers, arranged in such a way as to make many narrow winding paths, with seats placed at intervals, after the manner of alcoves.

'Where are you taking me?' asked Beatrice, shivering, she knew not why.

Casting a glance of undisguised admiration upon her lovely shoulders, her bosom white as driven snow, her bare arms, and her pretty face, he answered, while his voice trembled with a passion he either could not or did not care to conceal—

'My darling—for you must allow me to call you so —I have brought you here to tell you I love you. Nay, start not. Since the first moment I beheld you, my heart has been irrevocably yours. I felt that you were my fate, and I could not resist you. I knew that you were my goddess, and I could not help but worship you.'

'Oh, Sir Frederick!' cried Beatrice, who had listened to this appeal with breathless astonishment. 'This is so sudden—I am unprepared. For heaven's sake take me back to mamma!'

'Not until I have an assurance from your lips that you will return my affection.'

Beatrice made no reply.

Her bosom heaved and fell, her face, neck, and

shoulders became crimson, and then, as the hot tide
receded, she became deadly pale.

Employing just as much gentle violence as was
necessary, Sir Frederick Cazenove pressed her back
into a seat, and placing himself by her side, insinuated
his arm round her waist, drawing her close to his
side.

' Dearest,' he cried, in a clear, bell-like voice, which
was yet low and sweet, and which thrilled through her,
vibrating pleasantly upon the most sensitive chords of
her heart, ' dearest, you must—you shall listen to me.
I can contain myself no longer.'

Involuntarily she nestled closer to him, and allowed
her head to sink upon his shoulder, while she looked
up dreamily into his handsome, aristocratic face, every
feature of which was beaming with love for her.

' If you love me with the same wild, passionate, all-
sacrificing love I feel for you,' he continued, ' and I
can read your character and thoughts sufficiently well
to know that I am far from indifferent to you.'

Beatrice cast down her eyes in modest confusion.

' You are not justified in saying that,' she exclaimed,
' as I have as yet admitted nothing.'

' But it is true, Beatrice, my darling, my dearest,
my hope!' he cried, eagerly. ' You cannot deny it.
Come, then, let us fly this very night, and speed to
climes where our existence can be one dream of love.
My yacht——'

Beatrice disengaged herself with a jerk from his
clinging embrace.

Her eyes flashed with an indignant fire; her lips
were parted, and her bosom, which had before heaved
with a sensuous passion, now panted with rising rage.
His meaning was too plain to be mistaken.

' What!' she exclaimed, extending her right hand
as if to denounce him, ' you dare to talk of love, and in

the same breath have the hardihood to make me a proposition which involves my dishonour!'

'You mistake my meaning,' he answered, remaining perfectly calm beneath her fierce denunciation.

His unruffled demeanour rather inclined her to believe that she might have misunderstood him, and she listened in silence for his explanation.

'We can sail in my yacht for France, where we——'

She would listen no more.

'No, Sir Frederick,' she exclaimed, hurriedly, 'I can divine your meaning too well. The proposal you make to me is dishonourable in the extreme. I was weak and foolish just now. I am strong and well again, thank heaven, and entreat you to conduct me to the ball-room.'

'In what have I offended you?' he asked, rather puzzled what course to pursue.

'You professed to love me—what answer I might have been induced a little while ago to give you, in the infatuation of the moment, I don't know; but what can I think of a man who asks me to elope with him when there could not possibly be any impediment to a marriage?'

'I am romantic,' he answered, with a deep sigh; 'let that be my excuse for proposing anything of a clandestine nature. I have no objection whatever to demand your hand in a formal manner of your mother; will that satisfy you?'

'Perfectly,' replied Beatrice, after a moment's consideration.

She was naturally of a forgiving disposition, and felt only too pleased to receive his apology, for, with his gentle manners and handsome face, he had made an impression on her heart which she found it difficult to eradicate.

' We are good friends again ? ' he queried.

' I hope so.'

Offering her his arm he led her, suffused with blushes and smiles, to the ball-room. Guiding her to a seat he exclaimed—

' I will go and seek Mrs. Harrington if you will kindly remain here.'

' If any one should tempt me to dance ? '

' You must turn a deaf ear, and refuse to be tempted.'

' Oh, what tyrants you men are when you think you have acquired a little power over us ! ' exclaimed Beatrice.

He left her alone, and pretended to look for Mrs. Harrington, who, however, was snugly ensconced in the supper-room, devoting her attention partly to roast chicken and ham, and partly to the rather stale, and not altogether merited compliments paid her by her cavalier, who was solely actuated by a hope that, through ingratiating himself with the mother, he might stand a chance of an introduction to her lovely daughter.

When Sir Frederick Cazenove returned he said to Beatrice—

' Your mother is tired to death ; she declares she has been looking everywhere for you, and has just allowed me to place her in the carriage, where she now awaits your coming.'

' Indeed ! ' said Beatrice.

She did not suspect him of any sinister design, and jumped up with alacrity, adding—

' Poor dear mamma, I know she soon gets tired, and, to tell the truth, I feel a little knocked up.'

They had by this time reached the staircase, down which Sir Frederick hurried her, fearful lest Mrs. Harrington should meet them on the stairs, when of necessity all his plans would be discovered and frustrated.

Fortunately for himself, but unhappily for Beatrice, they did not encounter Mrs. Harrington. Beatrice went into the room where she had left her shawl, and throwing it over her shoulders accompanied Sir Frederick to the door, where his carriage was waiting, as she thought, to convey them to the Hermitage.

A black servant of Sir Frederick's, named Mustapha, wearing a turban, the short jacket and loose trousers which characterise the inhabitants of the East—a fellow half-Turk, half-Greek—opened the door of the carriage.

It was rather dark outside, and though the lamps shed a sickly glare in the road, Beatrice could see nothing distinctly, owing to the sudden change from a blaze of light to comparative darkness.

She had seen Mustapha before at the Hermitage, so that his appearance did not startle or surprise her in the least.

As soon as she was in the carriage Sir Frederick Cazenove sprang lightly after her, Mustapha jumped on the box beside the coachman, and the vehicle drove off at a quick pace.

For a moment Beatrice did not remark that her mother was absent from the carriage.

She had scarcely pulled up her dress and settled herself comfortably in a corner, when the fact burst upon her.

'Where—where—where's mamma?' she stammered.

'Pardon the deception I have had recourse to,' exclaimed Sir Frederick. 'I——'

'Oh, let us out!' cried Beatrice, now fearfully alarmed. 'I will get out! Such treatment is monstrous!'

She endeavoured to open the window, but twining

his strong arm around her he effectually prevented her from doing anything of the sort.

She raised her voice and began to scream, thinking that she should thereby call the attention of some belated passer-by to her desperate position, and obtain deliverance.

Sir Frederick drew her to him and stopped her cries with kisses, which she did her best to ward off.

' It is useless to resist,' he exclaimed, when she became a little calm. ' No harm will happen to you; why be so alarmed. I am not an ogre.'

' O, what will become of me ? ' cried Beatrice clasping her hands.

Her heart sank within her. She was completely in the power of a man whom she knew to be a libertine from what he had said to her that evening. By a stratagem he had taken her away from her only protector.

When the carriage reached the end of the street she found to her dismay that it turned to the west, and was going in a direction totally opposite to that of the Hermitage.

' What have I done that I should be treated thus ? ' she cried in a moaning voice.

' My dear child, do not give way to such excessive grief,' exclaimed Sir Frederick, compassionating her unmistakable distress.

' I cannot help it,' she sobbed.

Her fortitude gave way, and she had recourse to a woman's inevitable vent for an overburdened mind.

' I assure you that you have nothing to fear,' he said in a soothing voice. ' I love you very dearly, it is true, but that is an additional reason why I should treat you with kindness and consideration. " The Phryne " is moored under the cliffs. I shall take you on board, and we will sail to another land, where—'

'No, no, a thousand times no !' cried Beatrice, whom these words worked into a frenzy of excitement. ' Death is preferable to dishonour.'

'I intend you no dishonour,' he rejoined. ' We can procure a priest without any difficulty, who will make us man and wife.'

'I distrust you,' she replied. ' Why, if your intentions are fair and honourable, should you have recourse to this violence, as I told you in the ball-room my mother would have had no objection to the union ? '

'I detest anything formal.'

'That is an excuse. I am confident that you intend to ruin me ; but I warn you that death is preferable to dishonour. I will perish by my own hand, and if I can find no dagger, no knife wherewith to kill myself, I will plunge into the sea.'

'This passionate rage, darling, very much becomes you,' said Sir Frederick tauntingly ; 'you are very lovely. No knife would be so cruel as to pierce that fair skin, no sea so wicked as to drown you.'

The carriage drew up with a sudden jerk.

They had reached that particular part of the cliff where, by crossing the railway, and taking a winding path, they would reach the beach.

The town of Dover lay in repose on their left ; behind them was the dark country, stretching for many miles inland ; to the right, frowning majestically, was Shakespeare's Cliff ; before them extended the placid ocean, unruffled by the slightest breeze.

The ripple of the wavelets as they broke upon the pebbly beach was distinctly audible.

A short distance from the shore could be seen the ' Phryne.' A light was displayed at her bows, and a lantern, which moved with every undulation of the sea, indicated that a boat was waiting for the arrival of the profligate baronet and his beautiful victim.

Sir Frederick Cazenove sprang out of the carriage, and extended his hand to assist Beatrice to alight, taking it for granted that she would accompany him without any demur.

She descended from the carriage, but no sooner had her feet touched the ground, than she darted forward with the rapidity of lightning, and, eluding his grasp, disappeared in the darkness.

'Lights!' shouted Sir Frederick, foaming with rage. 'Lights here! The girl has escaped me. Mustapha, you black scoundrel! after her, sir!'

The black no sooner heard this command than he hastened in pursuit of Beatrice, who, as far as he could see in the hurry and confusion of the moment, had taken the direction of the cliff, and was ascending its precipitous side with the agility of a chamois.

The men in the boat, who were no other than Captain Hicks and Bowker, hastened over the beach and across the railway to the spot at which the carriage had stopped.

'What's the matter, Sir Frederick?' inquired Hicks.

On Bowker's face there was an expression of pleasure. He could guess what had happened. The driver, an old hand, and accustomed to these adventures of his master, sat still and stolid on his box, troubling himself about nothing but his horses.

'Matter, my good fellow!' replied Sir Frederick; 'matter enough. The cursed girl has got away after all my trouble.'

'In what direction?'

'Up the cliff; but it's so infernally dark that she may have doubled, and be making for the town. Do you, Hicks, go up the cliff and search for her; you, Bowker, had best go to the town and guard the road. She must be caught, or I shall have to make myself scarce in Dover for a time.'

The two men started off, each in a different direction, to obey their master's behest.

In the meantime Beatrice had pursued a path which led her up the cliff. She toiled laboriously to gain the summit, thinking that she was gaining on Sir Frederick and his myrmidons, and consoling herself with the reflection that she could throw herself over the cliff, and be dashed to pieces on the rocks below, if she were overtaken.

It was a very dark night; scarcely a star was to be seen. Now and then a phosphorescent glow broke out on the sea as a larger wave than usual disturbed its surface; but it was with the utmost difficulty, and, indeed, almost by a miracle, that she kept the path.

It was an awful reflection that one false step would precipitate her into eternity; but she had no time for thinking.

It was fortunate that it was so; had she enjoyed time and leisure for meditation, her brain would have temporarily given way, and she would have sank insensible on the ground, an easy prey to her would-be seducer.

At length she halted, thoroughly exhausted. Leaning forward, and straining her faculties to the utmost, she listened.

The heavy breathing of a man labouring up the steep hill fell upon her startled ears.

' Oh God ! ' she cried ; ' they are upon me ! '

Stepping forward wearily, she prepared to continue her flight.

She had not proceeded more than a dozen paces, however, before she felt the earth giving way beneath her feet.

Treading inadvertently, in the darkness of the night, upon a rotten part of the cliff, it had given way with her.

A despairing shriek broke from her as she felt herself

falling—falling like a rebellious angel hurled through space down to the bottomless pit by the divine wrath.

Her senses were leaving her.

Suddenly she struck with considerable violence against some hard substance.

Her fall was arrested.

Providentially, after falling a few feet, she had struck upon a projecting ledge of rock.

This accident, dreadful though it appeared, had saved her.

In another minute the black Mustapha, following her with the unerring instinct of a bloodhound, would have seized and dragged her with a wild glee to the vessel, hoping thereby to gain his master's good opinion, and receive a handsome reward.

She was not much hurt.

Fearing to move, lest she might topple over and perish on the rocks below, she remained perfectly still, anxiously awaiting the appearance of morning.

Mustapha, finding that his exertions were lamentably wasted, and that he was merely jeopardising his valuable neck in wandering up and down the cliff, returned to his master, whose rage, though still intense, had somewhat subsided.

'Well!' he ejaculated as the black appeared.

'I can see nothing of the lady, sir,' replied the black.

'That is strange,' said Sir Frederick Cazenove; 'can she have tumbled into the sea? Whatever her fate, I shall go on board the yacht and cruise in the channel until the evening, when two lights displayed as usual—green over blue—will bring me back.'

'Shall I remain on the watch?' inquired Mustapha.

'Yes,' said Sir Frederick; 'it may be productive of some good. Keep guard on the cliff unitl the morning.'

'If I should meet with the lady——'

'Conduct her at once and at all hazards to the Hermitage. See to this, and you shall have no cause to regret your zeal.'

The black bowed low.

Captain Hicks sounded a whistle, which had the effect of bringing Bowker to the scene of action.

'Follow me, Sir Frederick,' exclaimed Captain Hicks. 'The path to the beach is a little awkward to those unaccustomed to its tortuous windings.'

'Stand aside, man,' replied Sir Frederick, contemptuously ; 'if I don't know it as well as you, may I never plan another abduction.'

He was fond of speaking roughly and rudely to his dependants, and occasionally resorted to blows to further impress his meaning upon them.

The quietude which had up to the present time characterised the atmosphere no longer existed. For some hours dark banks of clouds had been drifting up from the southward, bringing a cold wind with them, a few drops of rain plashed upon the ground, and the crescent moon, rendered visible occasionally as the patches of ragged clouds swept past it, sufficed to show that the sea was heaving restlessly.

'A dirty night,' said the skipper, shaking his head ominously.

'That may or may not be,' observed Sir Frederick. 'If the wind rises, there may be a little swell on the shore, but we shall be safe enough in mid-channel.'

'I would rather run over to Calais, if you have no objection, Sir Frederick,' said Captain Hicks.

'You may go to the devil for what I care,' replied his gracious master; ''that is, provided you let me alone. When I'm on board I shall turn in, and I won't be disturbed on any account—not even if the sky falls or it rains little fishes.'

'It is to be hoped you will wake in a better temper,' muttered Captain Hicks, adding in a low tone to Bow-

L

ker—'I don't half like the look of the weather, and we'll cut right across and lie snug in Calais Harbour.'

'Ay, ay,' said Bowker ; 'I'm your man. It's some time since I said parley-voo to any one of your mossoos.'

'There was a little bit of a French girl, wasn't there? one of those——'

'Stow that, cappen!' cried Bowker getting red in face, and walking on ahead to conceal his confusion.

The party embarked on board the yacht, which was soon standing away from the shore in the track of the mail-steamer which had a short time before preceded them across the Channel.

Mustapha had a long and solitary vigil.

Captain Hick's predictions about the weather were not realised ; the wind shifted, the rain held up, and the stars came out.

The black was a faithful servant. Sir Frederick Cazenove did not rule him through fear. His obedience and unscrupulous fidelity to his master were prompted by love. Sir Frederick had saved Mustapha's life, under peculiar circumstances, during one of his journeys in the East, and ever since that day the life he saved had been devoted to his service.

On the top of the cliff was an old hut. It had probably served as a protection to the coast-guardsmen, but was in a terribly dilapidated condition. Its wretched timbers leant one against the other, and it was guiltless of a roof. It served, however, as a poor protection against the violence of the wind, and towards morning Mustapha, espying it, strolled in, leant against the side, and inadvertently went to sleep.

How long he slept he did not know, but when he woke it was broad daylight. Starting up with an oath, which did not become a good Moslem, he rubbed his eyes, and darted out on to the cliff.

A man and a boy were walking together on the verge. The man had a coil of rope in his hand, one end of which was fastened to a crowbar driven firmly into the earth.

Sauntering up to him, Mustapha looked on at his preparations, wondering what he was about to do.

The man was a samphire-gatherer. In order to obtain the little plant called samphire, he daily jeopardised the life of his son.

Without taking any notice of the black, he fastened the rope around his child's waist, and with great solicitude lowered him over the cliff.

In one hand the boy carried a basket of small dimensions, in the other a knife.

Suddenly the rope jerked.

' Hallo !' cried the man ; ' something wrong.'

And he began pulling up rapidly hand over hand.

Presently the boy's head appeared at the surface.

Hauling him on to the land, his father said—

' What's the matter, Johnny ?'

' About ten feet down, father, lying on a ledge of rock, is a woman, and she is so still and quiet, I think she is dying.'

At the mention of a woman, Mustapha listened attentively.

What if she should prove to be the missing lady of whom he was in search ?

His resolution was taken immediately.

The samphire-gatherer regarded his boy with astonishment.

' A woman, did you say ?' he exclaimed.

' Yes, father,' replied the lad.

' How is she dressed ?'

' Like a lady.'

' Oh '' exclaimed Mustapha, wringing his hands. ' Perhaps it is my poor dear mistress. She came on the cliff last night for a walk after the ball, and I have been searching for her ever since.'

' Your mistress, eh ! ' ejaculated the samphire-gatherer.

' Yes, my good man,' replied the black. ' You shall have gold—much gold—if you will bring her to the ground here.'

' I'll have your money if I earn it,' returned the man, ' though, for the matter of that, I would gladly save a fellow-creature's life for nothing. You must stand by the rope, and help the lad to haul up—first the lady, and then me. Stand firm, for the love of God. There must be no blundering or hesitation in this work, or it's just being pitched headlong into eternity, that's all.'

' And enough too,' said Mustapha. ' Never fear. Though my skin is a different colour from your own, I have some strength in my arms, and you need not be afraid to trust to me.'

' I'll risk it,' said the samphire-gatherer.

Setting his lips firmly together, he unfastened the rope from the lad's waist, and tied it round his own, giving Mustapha instructions the while how he should lower him over the cliff.

At length everything was ready, and he disappeared over the precipice, Mustapha paying out the rope little by little.

At length there was a jerk.

Some minutes elapsed, which appeared an age to those on the bank, so great was their anxiety to know whether the lady was alive or dead.

When the rope again jerked, Mustapha hauled it up slowly, so as to prevent the strain upon it causing the strands to snap.

Up, up, until the skirts of a white muslin dress was visible; up, until the inanimate body of a woman, and that woman Beatrice Harrington, was safely landed.

The samphire-gatherer had, with a courage beyond all praise, left himself on the ledge, entirely at the mercy of those above.

As soon as he could disengage the rope, Mustapha lowered it again. It was successfully caught by the samphire-gatherer, who in his turn was brought to the top of the cliff.

Mustapha now despatched the lad into the town for a fly. To carry Beatrice in his arms to the Hermitage was out of the question, and while awaiting the arrival of the carriage, he conversed with the samphire-gatherer, and gave him a sovereign which he had in his pocket.

Beatrice did not open her eyes. She seemed completely exhausted. The fact was, she had remained in her desperate position until her brain gave way. She was delirious with fear, and had not her senses left her she would probably have fallen over the side, and have died miserably.

When the fly came, Beatrice was placed in it, and driven to the Hermitage. She was carried to the old bedroom in which she had slept before, and laid on the bed, while Mustapha went to another part of the house and sought Mrs. Greaves, the housekeeper, to whom he briefly related what had occurred.

Mrs. Greaves listened with a frown upon her wrinkled brow.

' I wish,' she exclaimed, when the black had finished his recital, ' that Sir Frederick hated women as much as I do, then we shouldn't have the house continually turned topsy-turvy for the painted things. Tell Miss Maynard I want her.'

To find this lady Mustapha had to go to the west wing. Miss Maynard was a lady of about six-and-thirty years of age, with a pensive countenance. On making inquiries, he found she was in the garden, and there he spoke to her.

She went at once to Mrs. Greaves, and was briefly informed of the singular adventure of which Beatrice was the heroine, but refused to have anything to do with her detention.

'Heaven knows, Mrs. Greaves,' she exclaimed, 'that I have enough on my mind as it is. For seven years have I been—'

'Hush!' cried the housekeeper in a tone of alarm. 'It is dangerous to speak above your breath.'

'You know what I mean, so further explanation is not needed. I implore you, however, to manage this affair yourself. If you cannot do so, I will step in at the last moment; but I have a woman's repugnance to assist Sir Frederick in the execution of schemes which are too disgraceful and serious in their consequences to dwell upon.'

'It is always I who have to do everything,' said Mrs. Greaves in a passion, flouncing out of the room, and leaving Miss Maynard with Mustapha.

The lady heaved a deep sigh.

Mustapha was about to withdraw, when she beckoned him to her side.

'When this girl recovers,' she exclaimed, 'let me know. I will visit her.'

'Yes, miss,' replied Mustapha.

Then Miss Maynard retired to the west wing, and busied herself in duties which are of no interest to the reader.

When Beatrice came to herself, she fancied she was dreaming. Back again in the old Hermitage! It could not be. Was she able to credit the evidence of her senses?

Mrs. Greaves had been watching her, and that lady's

harsh voice soon persuaded her that she was not in the land of spirits.

' So you are awake at last, young lady!' she exclaimed. ' Don't look so scared. This is the house you were visiting a short time back. Your mamma left this morning in great disgust, thinking you had eloped with Sir Frederick, and is now at the Lord Warden, in Dover, sending telegrams to different parts, communicating with the detective police, and lamenting that she didn't make you a ward in Chancery.'

' How did I come here?' asked Beatrice, still bewildered.

' Mustapha brought you.'

' But the cliff—I can hear the shrill cries of the sea-mew, the howl of the wind, the wash of the sea on the rocks below. O God, the horror of that night!'

' According to the black's account, you were drawn up from your perilous position by a samphire-gatherer.'

' May I not go and join my mother?' exclaimed Beatrice. ' Believe me, I feel deeply grateful to all of you for your kindness.'

' Sir Frederick's permission must be obtained before you can be allowed to quit this house,' answered Mrs. Greaves.

' Sir Frederick! where is he?'

' Never mind; perhaps he will be here quite soon enough for you.'

' That is an additional reason,' said Beatrice, earnestly, ' why you should assist me to escape. He has made dishonourable proposals to me.'

' I can readily believe that,' returned Mrs. Greaves, with a grim smile, ' and I can tell you that you are not the first, by some dozens, he has treated in the same way, if that is any consolation to you.'

The mocking tone in which the woman spoke made the girl's blood run cold.

'Are—are you serious?' she gasped.

'There is never much in this house to make me anything else. Make up your mind to stay here. I will send you up another dress, so that you can make yourself look decent.'

And, as if to prevent any further conversation, she abruptly left the room. A housemaid soon afterwards brought her some articles of wearing apparel, and when she had made her toilette, a small but substantial repast, for which she was very grateful, was sent to her on a tray.

Deeply meditating, Beatrice sat in the sitting-room which had been provided for her.

All at once her privacy was intruded upon by Mustapha, who ushered in Miss Maynard.

There was something in this lady's face which served to reassure Beatrice.

Obeying an instinctive impulse she sprang forward and seized her by the hand, exclaiming,

'I do not know who you are nor whence you come, but something tells me you are a friend, and mean to deliver me.'

'Indeed, you are greatly mistaken,' replied Miss Maynard. 'I intend to do nothing of the sort.'

Beatrice's countenance fell.

A peculiar look, however, with which Miss Maynard favoured her, served to reassure her a little.

Mustapha was standing near the door watching the two ladies with curious eyes.

'You can withdraw,' exclaimed Miss Maynard.

He salaamed and withdrew at once.

When they were alone, she exclaimed in an eager voice,

'My dear girl, you judged correctly—I am your

friend, but this house is so full of spies and secrets, that it is dangerous to speak above one's breath. I came with the intention of delivering you from a fate to which death is preferable.'

'Who are you?' asked Beatrice.

'Ask me not. I can only tell you that I am what I trust you may never be,' replied Miss Maynard sadly.

' Pardon so rude a question. It was only put with the object of learning to whom I was indebted for so much unmerited kindness.'

' Not unmerited. You are a woman, and in distress. I came here to succour you ; put on your bonnet, and follow me.'

' I have none. You forget, or you have not heard, that I was at a ball last night.'

' It had escaped my memory ; take my own. We do not study the fashions here, but you will find it serviceable. My jacket too is at your service. Do not tarry. The servants are at tea, and I wish to get you away from here before Sir Frederick returns.'

' Then he is not at present an inmate of the Hermitage ? '

' No, he is at sea in his yacht, so Mustapha informs me.'

The transference of the bonnet and jacket was soon accomplished, and Beatrice was successfully conducted into the garden, and from thence guided out of the grounds by her kind friend and ally.

' We must part here,' said Miss Maynard.

' Thanks, thanks; a thousand thanks !' exclaimed Beatrice, affected almost to tears. ' If we must part, at least do not stifle the new-born friendship I feel springing up in my heart. Tell me to whom I am indebted?'

' I am called Cora,' replied Miss Maynard ; ' and if ever you should return to this house—'

' Never—never !'

' Be not too sure.   Sir Frederick Cazenove is one of those remarkably pertinacious men who never abandon a promised pleasure.   It is far from improbable that you will visit the Hermitage again.   If I should unhappily prove a true prophet, remember that Cora will always be your friend.'

Beatrice smiled incredulously.

Kissing Miss Maynard on each cheek, she took her leave, and then walked quickly in the direction of Dover, which she reached in about an hour.

She found that the waiters and the other loungers about the hotel regarded her strangely, and whispered among themselves as she approached.

Taking no notice of them, she walked upstairs and entered the sitting-room which had been occupied by her mother and herself.

Mrs. Harrington was seated at a table penning a despatch, or rather writing a letter, to her solicitors, the Messrs. Burt, respecting the elopement of her daughter.

As the door opened, she uttered a cry of astonishment.

To see her daughter back again was indeed a surprise, as she fully believed she had eloped with Sir Frederick Cazenove; and she had industriously noised the report all over Dover, saying to herself, ' He must marry her when the thing is made so public.'

' Is it you, Beatrice ?' she exclaimed.   ' Where is your husband ?'

' What on earth do you mean, mamma ?' replied Beatrice.

' You went away with Sir Frederick Cazenove last night.   I have witnesses to prove it ; and if you come back four-and-twenty hours afterwards, you return to me dishonoured.'

' Hear my story, and you will alter your opinion.'

' I can listen to nothing !' hastily interrupted Mrs. Harrington. ' The most romantic story in the world would be no palliation of—'

' But I insist upon it,' said Beatrice, stamping her foot imperatively on the floor ; ' after what you have said, I have a right to demand to be heard.'

Finding her daughter resolute, Mrs. Harrington consented to hear her story. When she had concluded, she said in a low voice, and with a crestfallen air—

' I am bound to believe you, and after what has happened, the only admission I can make is, that I have made a fool of myself. We must leave Dover immediately.'

' And go—'

' To—to Italy—anywhere. I would go to Jericho if I thought this foolish affair would be unknown there. The packet leaves in an hour. Let us hasten to put our things together.'

In an hour and a half from that time the Harringtons were on their way to France.

Sir Frederick Cazenove and Beatrice never met again. The Harringtons remained abroad for some years, and when they returned to England, the match-making mother had the satisfaction of knowing that her daughter had changed her name, and that those who would have smiled at that of Beatrice Harrington could say nothing to that of the Countess Della Spada, which she had acquired through marrying the wealthy nobleman who bore that title.

The second attempt succeeded better than the first. But then, after all, these things require a little practice.